PROMISE

CHERISH AMORE

B. LOVE PUBLICATIONS

To my dear best friend Tijuana (TT), this book is dedicated to you. I love you more than I can ever express! Our friendship has been strong for the last twenty-three years and love has it been amazing —four kids between the two of us and a marriage apiece. Whew, child, it's been real, LOL! You're a strong individual, and I don't think you ever realize how strong you are. Your love for people is beyond amazing, and I don't think you get enough credit for how huge of a heart you have. I am honored to call you my best friend, and life wouldn't be half of what it is without you. I love you, bestie.

Ps. Thank you for sticking around when I would bully you when were in the fifth grade, LOL! Man, I was young and dumb. I love you, girl!

This one is for you.

ACKNOWLEDGMENTS

To my Lord and Savior, I say thank you first. Without Him, I wouldn't be here today.

To my amazing mother, thank you for continuously having my back and even reading my books, though I feel so weird, LOL!

Thank you so much B. Love. I enjoy being a part of the B.Love Publications family. I thank you for the daily knowledge you pour into me. You push me to perfect my craft.

Thank you to my pen sisters and brothers. You all are amazing.

To my dear friend, Teairrah, girl, we rocking out another one. I promise when I become rich like you claim I am, insider, we going to be rich together!

To my amazing supporters, as always, thank you! I have come so far from 2013 to now, and to still have y'all rocking with me is the best feeling ever. I am thankful for each one of you.

Let's ride this wave one more time.

A NOTE TO MY READERS

As always, thank you so for supporting me. Whether you purchased it or downloaded from Kindle Unlimited, know that each one of you are greatly appreciated. Writing has always been my passion, so being able to pen my feelings to paper and have support is an extraordinary feeling that will never go unnoticed, nor will the feeling leave.

Writing *Promise* was very special to me because, though the events that takes place in this book did not happen to me, there are so many others it has happened to. My heart aches for anyone that has every endured this pain or may still be enduring this pain. This masterpiece contains child abuse, drug abuse, explicit scenes, and profanity. If, for any reason, any of the above triggers you, I respectfully ask that you not continue with this read. Also, again, this is a work of fiction. Though things in this book may resemble real life situations for some, this book was solely written from my imagination.

If you do decide to continue, I truly hope you enjoy reading this as much as I did writing this book.

As always, my loves, happy reading!

Cherish Amore

February 8th, 2011

Promise sat outside on the cold, wooden bench as she waited patiently for the stranger to arrive. *Relax, Promise, you have waited forever this,* she thought as she rubbed her sweaty hands on her denim jeans.

She had already been waiting for almost thirty minutes, and though she was early, she was now becoming impatient because the person she was meeting was now late.

"I don't even know why I bothered," Promise whispered with sadness in her voice after checking her iPhone.

The time displayed 3:35 p.m.; the person was now thirty-five minutes late. A slight pain ran through her chest as she stood to her feet. Even after all these years, things were still the same.

"Promise?" she heard her name faintly just as she was walking away from the bench, and she slowly turned around.

"Promise Lewis?" she heard. She almost said no because she hadn't gone by Lewis since she was ten years old.

"Yes?" she answered. Her voice was shaky, and tears began to form.

"I'm Promise," she said, staring at the lady as her body began to shiver involuntarily as if she was cold.

"Oh… my… gosh…" the lady spoke slowly as she walked toward Promise before hugging her tightly once she reached her.

Promise wanted so badly to hug her back, but she couldn't bring herself to do it. She even wanted the hug to feel warm and safe, but it was everything but warm and safe.

"I'm sorry," the woman spoke, releasing Promise from the hug before wiping her tears. "Would you like to sit?" the woman asked, gesturing to the bench that Promise had just got up from.

Hell no! Promise wanted to scream, but instead, she nodded her head before walking toward the bench and sitting.

"You're just like I always imagined. You're beyond stunning." The woman complimented her.

Promise only stared at her with tears burning the rim of her eyelids. However, she refused to let them fall.

"I am so glad you found me. I had been trying to find you for years," the woman continued.

I can't do this, Promise thought.

"Why did you abandon me?" she blurted out, looking at the woman as if she was crazy.

"I didn't ask to be in this world," Promise continued.

"I was your child, yet you threw me away as if I was trash," she added as she became angry.

"Ten years old, and you threw me away like I didn't mean a thing to you." She raised her voice while standing from the bench, feeling as though coming to meet this woman was a big mistake.

"How could you?" Promise questioned as she turned her

back to the woman, unable to hold the tears back but refused to let her see her cry.

"How could you do that to your own flesh and blood?" she questioned with her back still to the woman as she thought back to everything leading up to this moment.

Chapter One

August 18th, 1986

"Ahhh!" seventeen-year-old Jennifer Lewis screamed as the doctor inserted his fingers into her vagina to see how many centimeters dilated she was; she was having a contraction at the same time.

"Please stop," she whined as she clenched her legs, trying to close them.

"Ms. Lewis, in order for me to check you properly, I am going to need you to open your legs. Just take deep, slow breaths," the doctor said, already growing tired of Jennifer.

"How about I stick my hand up your—"

"Jennifer!" her mother scolded, cutting her words short because she had a good idea on what her daughter was going to say.

"Just relax." Her mother encouraged, and Jennifer closed her eyes tightly and did just that.

"Alright. You're at five centimeters," he announced once

he removed his hands from Jennifer's vagina before removing the sterile gloves and tossing them in the trash.

"At this point in your labor, I do suggest you get the epidural because if you can't take me checking you, you surely won't be able to handle pushing a baby out naturally," he said with an attitude before walking out of the room without waiting for a reply.

"It's almost over, baby girl," Jennifer's mother, Cynthia, said as she placed the cold washcloth she had been holding onto her daughter's forehead, trying to soothe her.

"Ma, you said that twenty-four hours ago," Jennifer whined.

"I know I did, but at least now you're at five centimeters versus the three centimeters you were for a long time," she said. "Also, I agree with the doctor. You should get the epidural. It will allow you to sleep, and you won't feel the pain."

"Yeah, I want it!" she damn near shouted.

At first, Jennifer thought she would be a trooper and push her baby out with no medicine, but after twenty-four hours and all the damn pain, that plan went out the window.

"Go get the doctor, Mama. Tell him I want it! Tell someone out there I want the epidural!" she cried.

Cynthia went in search of someone as she silently prayed the baby would come soon and her baby would no longer be in pain.

IT HAD BEEN another twenty-four hours, and Jennifer was finally fully dilated and trying to push her daughter out into the world. She had been pushing for almost an hour.

"Ahh! I can't do this!" Jennifer cried as tears ran down her face. "Just give me a C-section already!" she begged.

"Absolutely not!" the doctor said firmly.

"I can see her head, so you're going to push her out," he added.

The doctor may not have been the nicest, but he was good at his job.

"Now, push," he said once Jennifer started having another contraction.

"Harder! That's right! Harder, harder!" He encouraged.

Jennifer was running out of air. She was tired, and the medicine was wearing off. She was determined this baby had to get the hell out of her now.

"Ahh!" she screamed as she pushed with everything she had in her.

Pushing one more time, she gave it her all. Seconds later, she heard a powerful yet sweet cry.

"It's a girl," the doctor announced dryly.

"Jennifer, she is beautiful," Cynthia cried as she cut the umbilical cord.

It was a good thing Cynthia was there to support her daughter. Jennifer didn't have anyone else since her baby's father was killed in a car accident three months ago.

"Congratulations," the doctor said, not even a little bit enthused, after he had finished up with Jennifer before walking out her room.

"Here you go, mom," the friendly nurse said as she handed Jennifer her swaddled baby girl.

The moment Jennifer took her baby girl from the nurse, she began crying. She looked like her daddy. With a head full of curly, jet-black hair, beautiful, golden skin, a tiny button nose, chubby cheeks, ten perfect fingers, and ten wiggly toes, she was simply perfect.

"I love you already," Jennifer whispered.

"Your daddy would have loved you so much," she added, looking down at her beautiful creation.

"What's her name?" the nurse asked, interrupting the moment.

"Promise Love Lewis," Jennifer said, never looking up from her daughter.

Originally, Jennifer hated the name, but that's what Promise's father wanted to name her, so she fulfilled his wishes.

"That is beautiful," the nurse said with a smile.

Jennifer had labored for forty-eight hours with almost two hours of pushing, but none of that or anyone else mattered anymore. She had her beautiful little angel that she would forever love.

Two

June 7th, 1995

"Promise, move it before we miss this damn bus!" Jennifer yelled at her daughter as she power walked in front of her, headed to the bus stop.

"Mommy, I'm trying," Promise whined, jogging behind her mother, her little legs in overdrive as the barrettes on her long pigtails hit her in the eye with each step.

"Dammit! We missed the bus!" she shouted when she noticed the number nine bus pulling off from the curb the second they turned the corner.

"I told your ass to come the hell on!" Jennifer turned around, yelling at Promise.

"It's your damn fault!" she scolded before raising her hand, smacking Promise to the ground.

"Told your ass to come on, man," she added, huffing.

"Now get your ass up before I beat you in these streets!" she shouted.

Promise's silent tears fell from her eyes as she stood to

her feet, brushing herself off. Truth was, it wasn't her fault they were late, Jennifer woke up late and then tried to rush Promise out of the house.

"Sorry," she muttered.

Promise was now eight years old, and her life was a living hell. Jennifer would beat on Promise for no reason, and when she drank, it was worse. It didn't get this way until Cynthia passed away two years go.

"Come on. Now we gotta wait." Jennifer roughly grabbed Promise's small hand, dragging her to the bench at the bus stop.

"Sit down," she ordered, and Promise did as she was instructed without so much of a peep or eye blink.

"Aye, sweetcakes, why you lookin' so mean?" a guy in a black Monte Carlo asked as he pulled alongside the curb of the bus stop.

Jennifer didn't answer. Instead, she stood there with her arms folded across her chest, looking up and down the street for a bus she knew she missed.

"You done missed that bus, sweetcakes. Next one ain't for another hour," he said, though Jennifer hadn't said a word to him.

"I know," she said, sucking her teeth, just wanting the dude to get out her face.

"Where ya headed? I can give you a ride," he offered with a smile.

Normally, Jennifer would have said "hell nah" and "carry your ass on", but because Promise couldn't be late to school anymore—because Jennifer would have to show up in court if she was—she went against what she normally would.

"The elementary school on Main Street." Her arms were still folded, but now she looked inside his car.

"Come on, you and ya lil' shorty. Come on. I got cha," the man offered.

"Let's go, Promise," she said, turning to Promise without a second thought.

"You get in this car and don't say not one word," she warned once Promise was near her.

"Thank you. I really appreciate it," she said to the man, her tone a lot calmer and sweeter than when she was talking to her own daughter.

"No sweat," he said, pulling off from the curb.

"So what's your name?" he casually asked, occasionally looking over at her.

"What's your name?" she asked with attitude. She wasn't feeling giving him her name, even if he was giving her a ride.

"My name is Steven, but everybody calls me Slick." He chuckled.

"Now you gon' tell me your name?" he asked once he stopped at a red light, peering over at her briefly.

"It's Jennifer," she revealed after slight hesitation.

"What's ya shorty name, Jennifer?" he asked, referring to Promise as he looked at her through the rearview mirror.

"You sure do ask a lot of questions," she said, becoming defensive, thinking that maybe he wanted to do harm to Promise.

"My bad, sweetcakes. Just making conversation," he admitted.

"Well, make conversation about me, not my child."

"Right." He nodded slowly.

"Well, where ya man at, Jennifer?" Slick asked, not beating around the bush.

"Who says I have a man?" she fired back while leaning on the door, facing him.

"You too damn fine not to."

Slick was right; Jennifer was fine. Jennifer was five feet eight with long, sexy, slender legs and hips for days, copper-colored skin, long, curly hair, and a smile that would lure anyone in. She was told a lot that she should be a model.

"Yeah, well, fine or not, I don't have a man," she huffed just as he pulled in front of Promise's school.

"I 'preciate the ride," she said, hopping out before letting the seat up so Promise could climb out.

"Come on. We already late, damn." She rushed Promise.

"You staying in the school all day with ya shorty?" he asked, looking over at her.

"Nah. I'ma take her up in there, then catch the bus back home," she announced as she grabbed Promise's hand to head inside.

"You ain't gotta catch the bus, sweetcakes. I'ma wait for you. Take ya time," Slick said, winking his eye at her when she turned around briefly.

That was the first day Promise met Steven, aka Slick, but this wouldn't be the last she saw of him. In fact, that was the start of a major life change for her because of him.

Chapter Three

December 1st, 1995

"Okay, class. Today's writing assignment will be a fun activity," Mrs. Dunkin spoke to her fourth-grade class as she stood in front of them.

"You guys are to write one hundred words or more saying what you would like for Christmas. You must also say why you would like those things for Christmas," she said.

I just want my mommy back to myself, nine-year-old Promise thought as she reached into her desk, pulling out her composition notebook and a number two pencil.

Jennifer wasn't so nice after Promise's big ma, Jennifer's mom, died. Once she got with Slick, she went from bad to worse. Promise never told anyone, but there were times that the only meal she had was when she came to school and ate lunch, and if it was the weekend, she was lucky to get a drink of water.

"Class, make sure you guys take your time with your spelling," Mrs. Dunkin said before sitting down at her desk.

"Also write neat and clear," she added.

Promise nervously looked around the room as all her classmates quickly began writing, all chipper and excited.

"Is there something wrong, Promise?" Mrs. Dunkin questioned in a concerned tone, looking right at Promise.

"No, ma'am," Promise mumbled, opening her composition book, unsure of what to write.

I don't want a doll, or new skates or even play-doh, Promise thought. *I really just want me and my mommy to be back like we used to be,* she thought just as she began her writing assignment.

December 01st, 1995
Mrs. Dunkin's Class
4th grade

Promise Lewis

MOST KIDS *my age are asking for skates, a new doll, a bike, a Game Boy, or maybe a Tamagotchi. Not me. For Christmas this year, I would just like to have my mother give me a hug and tell me that she loves me. It would be nice to get toys, but I think a warm hug from my mommy would be the best gift I could get this year. Also, if it was possible, I would like for my mommy's boyfriend, Uncle Slick, to leave us alone, because ever since he has come around, it hasn't been nice, and my mommy is different. That is all I want for Christmas.*

"Time's up, class. It's time for lunch," Mrs. Dunkin said just as Promise was finishing up her last sentence.

"Everyone, bring your composition notebooks to the front as you line up," she added.

Promise was happy it was lunchtime. Her stomach was

growling, and today, the cafeteria was serving her favorite
—pizza.

———————

MRS. DUNKIN SAT at her desk eating her lunch while reading
over her students' assignment. For the most part, they all said
the same thing—they wanted toys and more toys—until she
got to Promise's notebook.

"Oh my gosh," she whispered as she felt hot tears staining
her face.

Promise was always a good student, very quiet, polite,
and the top student in her class. One would never think she
had problems at home.

"Hey, Laura." The gym teacher, Robert interrupted in a
cheerful tone.

"I'm sorry I didn't mean to interrupt you…" He started
but stopped when he noticed the tears.

"Everything okay?" he asked in a concerned tone, walking
closer to his wife; she just hadn't changed her last name yet.

"Read this." Her words came out in a high-pitched tone
because she couldn't stop the tears.

"Wow," was all he could respond with once he was done
reading.

"I have to do something," she said.

"Baby, what are you going to do? It's no sign that she is
being harmed," he said, whispering when he called her
"baby", making sure no students would hear if they were
walking by.

"I don't know, but I have to do something," she mumbled.

"Something is just not right," she added.

"You can't interfere just because a little girl says she
would rather have a hug than toys, Laura," he said, knowing

his wife had a big heart and sometimes was over the top because she cared so much.

Just as she was about to respond, her class was being walked back from lunch by the cafeteria monitor in a single-file line.

"I'm sure she's fine," he whispered as he backed out of the classroom.

She had heard her husband, but she wasn't one to let things go. She would get to the bottom of it.

"PROMISE, could you stay back for a few moments?" Mrs. Dunkin asked as the rest of her students filed out of the classroom for recess.

Oh no. What did I do wrong? Promise thought nervously.

"Yes, ma'am. Am I in trouble?" she asked politely.

"Oh, sweetie. No, you're not in trouble," she replied, wanting nothing more than to embrace her and give her that warm hug she was yearning for from her mother.

"Is everything okay at home?" she questioned.

"Ummm…" Promise mumbled as she looked to the ground fiddling with her fingers.

Everything wasn't okay at home, but her mother threatened her daily that if she ran her mouth about what happened under her roof, she would have to pay.

"Yes," she whispered without looking up.

"Are you sure?" Mrs. Dunkin asked, raising her brow. "If something is going on, you can tell me."

I want to tell you so bad, but I can't, Promise thought.

Promise was only nine years old, but she was one of the smartest nine-year-olds anyone would cross.

"Everything is fine, Mrs. Dunkin," Promise assured with a false smile plastered on her beautiful face.

"Okay…" she dragged.

She could tell something wasn't right, but if Promise wasn't going to tell her, she couldn't help her.

"Go ahead outside with your friends. But if you ever want to talk, don't hesitate," she added.

"Okay. Yes, ma'am," Promise said before quickly turning around and heading outside.

Though Promise said everything was okay, Mrs. Dunkin followed her intuition and had to do something.

Little did she know, she was only making things worse.

———

PROMISE SLOWLY WALKED into the two-bedroom apartment that once only housed her and her mother, but now, Slick had become a permanent resident. Promise wished she could be in school 24/7.

Whap!

The second Promise pushed the front door open, she was smacked to the ground.

"What I told your ass about going to school to them uppity folks running your mouth about what goes on up in my shit?" Jennifer shouted as she held the belt that she had just hit Promise with.

"Mommy, I didn't say anything," Promise cried, holding the side of her face where the belt stung her at.

"You ain't say nothing, huh?" Jennifer questioned as she raised the belt and brought it down just as quickly, hitting Promise on her side, causing her to cry in pain upon connection.

"You got your fucking teacher calling my phone and shit, talking about an essay you wrote and shit, making me look like a bad person!" she continued yelling as she brought the belt down, hitting Promise twice more.

"Mommy!" she cried as she balled up in the fetal position trying not to get hit in the face.

"I didn't tell her anything, Mommy," she continued crying.

"You told the bitch something because why else would her ass call here?" Jennifer asked, a little out of breath from hitting Promise.

"I-I-I don't know," Promise stuttered through her cry.

"Get cho ass up out my damn face!" she shouted but not before hitting Promise two more times, one of which hit her in the eye and caused her to yell out in pain.

"And shut that fucking noise up before I fuck you up some more," she said, speaking to Promise as if she was some chick in the streets and not her nine-year-old daughter.

Promise quickly grabbed up her book bag that had fallen as she scurried to her room, still crying and now holding her eye that was stinging with pain and beginning to swell.

"I keep telling your ass you need to send her ass away, baby, because if you don't, she gon' cause a whole lot of trouble," Slick said as he sat on the sofa, bagging up his heroin and crack cocaine.

Slick was a local drug dealer, and sadly, he had gotten Jennifer hooked on the drugs, so she did whatever he said as long as he provided the drugs for free.

"I'ma have to do something," Jennifer said, secretly feeling bad for treating her daughter the way she had, but she would never tell anyone that.

"Come here, baby, and come get this hit. I know your ass tired from whipping her bad ass." Slick chuckled, his voice deep and powerful.

Jennifer's eyes lit up when she saw the crack pipe. She quickly dropped the belt and damn near ran to Slick's side. Slick didn't mess with his product, but he didn't give a fuck that Jennifer did since he was the one that got her hooked.

"Ow, ow, ow," Promise cried as she slowly sat on her air mattress that was barely inflated.

"God, why do I keep getting punished?" she whispered as she continued crying silent tears.

Promise didn't know what she ever deserved to get the treatment she received, but even after the physical and mental abuse, she loved her mother and wanted nothing more than for her to love her back.

Chapter
Four

December 25th, 1995

It was Christmas Day. Promise had been on Christmas break from school for two whole days now, but she wanted badly to be at school. She hadn't eaten since her last day at school before break, and her stomach was growling loudly.

Looking out her window, Promise could see all the little kids playing on their new bikes, skates, or playing with their remote-control cars while some little girls were pushing play strollers with their new dolls in them.

Without trying, Promise smiled. Even though her life was fucked up, she smiled for all the happy boys and girls her age.

"Get out that damn window looking all crazy," Jennifer slurred when she walked into Promise's room with a bottle of gin in her hand. It was only 9:30 in the morning.

"Yes, ma'am," Promise whispered.

It was funny how Jennifer didn't have an ounce of manners in her, no matter who she was talking to, but

Promise on the other hand was always respectful, no matter who she was talking to or how she was spoken to.

"Merry Christmas, Mommy!" Promise beamed as she reached under the wrinkly air mattress, pulling out the gift she had made at school.

"Shit. Christmas?" Jennifer drunkenly questioned, looking down at the handmade picture frame that had a picture of her and Promise in it.

"I didn't even know today was Christmas," she admitted.

Truth was, Jennifer didn't know half the days of the week, let alone holidays, because she was always drunk or high or both.

"This is so nice," she said as she swayed, preventing herself from falling.

"Thank you," she said, finally taking the picture frame from Promise, and Promise could actually hear some sadness in her voice.

"You're welcome, Mommy."

Promise was so happy her mother was a little happy about the gift she spent three days making in art class before she thought it was perfect.

"Promise, mommy was a little tight on money this year, so baby, I wasn't able to get you anything," Jennifer mumbled but felt extremely bad that she was so far gone she didn't even realize it was Christmas.

"It's okay, Mommy," she whispered.

Promise knew she wasn't getting a thing. Hell, they didn't even have a Christmas tree up, and most days, her mother barely spoke to her or whipped her ass, so she wasn't expecting anything.

"I really do love this." Jennifer examined the picture frame with tears now in her eyes.

"Where you get this picture?" she asked, looking down at the picture of when Promise was maybe about four; probably the last time the two of them had even taken a picture together.

"Grandma Cyn gave it to me before she died," Promise said with sadness, really missing her grandmother because had she been alive, things wouldn't be the way they were now.

"Aw, Pro—" Jennifer started just as she was going toward Promise to hug her.

"Baby, come on. I got ya shit ready," Slick mumbled, interrupting the moment as he stood in the doorway, holding up the mirror that had six perfectly straight lines of pure cocaine on it.

"I'm coming, daddy," Jennifer slurred as she quickly turned around, dropping the picture in the process.

"I knew you would be," Slick said with a smirk, looking at Promise as he slowly closed the door.

Slick knew what he was doing. He was always jealous of Promise and Jennifer's relationship, though he would never admit it. He knew drugs would win her over every time.

Tears now burned the rims of Promise's eyes. She was just about to get that hug she had written about, and for one second, her mom was actually about to act like the mother Promise needed. As always, Slick ruined it.

Picking up the picture frame slowly, the tears that burned her eyelids fell fast and hard.

"It was almost a perfect day," Promise whispered through her tears.

She stared at the picture, remembering a time when she and her mother were inseparable. Now, they barely were connected.

Promise just knew she would get that hug, and it was so close because she saw the look in her mother's eyes as she walked toward her, but like every other day, she was disappointed.

Chapter Five

August 17th, 1996

Nothing for Promise had changed one bit. As a matter of fact, things may have gotten worse. It was one day before Promise's tenth birthday, and though she knew she wasn't getting a thing, just like Christmas last year, she was still excited.

"Mommy, I will be ten tomorrow," she said excitedly, but Jennifer didn't say a word as she sat on the couch, biting her nails nervously.

"Did you hear me? I will be ten tomorrow," she repeated.

Still nothing.

"Mommy?" she said, sitting next to her on the couch.

"What, girl?" she yelled, still biting her nails.

"Nothing, Mommy." Sadness could be heard in her voice.

"You ready?" Slick asked when he walked out of their room with a Black & Mild hanging out of his mouth.

Jennifer didn't answer him either.

"I said are you ready?" he asked a little louder.

"Yeah," she mumbled.

Truth was, Jennifer wasn't ready. In fact, she was pretty much being forced to do something she didn't want to, but if she expected life to be better, she had to.

"Then let's go," he grumbled, walking past her on the sofa heading out the door.

"Come on, Promise," she dryly said, getting off the sofa.

Promise wanted to ask where they were going, but she was smart enough not to, because it would have probably led to her getting hit.

PROMISE FELT like she had been in the car forever, though it had actually been only an hour. She was ready to get to wherever they were going because she really had to pee. She wouldn't ask them to stop, because they would have told her she should have peed at home.

Finally, Promise thought as the car came to a complete stop. She could finally go pee.

"It's the right thing to do," she heard Slick say as he lit his Black & Mild cigar.

Jennifer didn't say anything to him as she climbed out of the car, just standing there for a few seconds before hitting the latch on the seat to let the seat up.

"Promise, come on," she mumbled.

Something wasn't right.

Without a word, Promise did as she was instructed and climbed out the back seat. Her hair bow snagged and came off from the seat belt getting caught on it.

"Leave it," Jennifer snapped.

"Mommy, you're hurting me," she cried as her mother held her hand tightly while pulling her to the side of the building they had pulled up to.

"Promise…" Jennifer started her voice cracking once they were on the side of the building.

"I was never supposed to be a single mother," she said, referring to Promise's father dying before she was born.

"And I damn sure wasn't supposed to raise you without my mother being around," she continued as tears started to fall, confusing Promise.

"I am only doing this because I love you," she added.

"Mommy, what's wrong?" Promised questioned, hating seeing her mother cry.

"He don't want you around, Promise. He takes care of me," she said.

Promise was still confused.

"Go into the police station, tell them your mother dropped you off, and you don't know where she went. Don't tell them where we live—nothing—and don't look back," she said. "You can't stay with us anymore, Promise. You just can't."

"Mommy—" Promise started, but her words were cut short.

"I mean it, Promise!" she shouted.

"Don't tell them shit." She roughly pulled Promise into a tight hug, kissing her chubby cheeks.

"I love you, Promise, but he don't want you around," she added before quickly turning to run back to the car without looking back at Promise.

Before she knew it, the car pulled off with her mother inside.

For thirty minutes, Promise just stood there just knowing her mother was coming back to get her, but when she didn't see any signs of her, she headed inside the police station.

"Can I help you, sweetheart?" the nice, blonde lady at the desk greeted the second Promise stepped inside.

"Are you alone?" she questioned, looking behind Promise.

Promise simply nodded her head with tears in her eyes. The officer at the desk said something into her walkie-talkie attached near her shoulder before coming around the counter near Promise.

"Where are your parents, sweetheart?" she asked.

"My mommy left me" she cried.

"I don't know where she went, but she left me," she continued, crying.

"It's okay, sweetheart. It's okay," the police officer said and pulled Promise close to her.

Even though she said it was okay, she knew it wasn't. Children were dropped off all the time by parents who no longer wanted to parent.

Chapter

Six

November 1st, 1996

I t had been almost three months since Promise was left
outside the police station, and though Jennifer told her
not to tell them where she lived, she did anyway. It was
no use though because the apartment was as empty as a
fridge in the hood before the first of the month.

The first night after being left in the police station,
Promise had to sleep in the station until Child Protective
Services arrived the next morning, and since then she had
been to three different houses. She was now residing at the
home of Marilyn and Joseph Montgomery. They were high
school sweethearts and got married right after.

Marilyn was a vice president of human resources for a
local company, and Joseph used to be a professional football
player until his career was ruined after a horrible injury. He
ran a successful trucking company. Because of the accident,
Joseph couldn't have any biological children, but that didn't
stop them from looking into adoption.

"Promise, honey, dinner is ready," Marilyn said sweetly.

When Promise first came to their home, she barely talked and acted out a lot because she was either mistreated or not paid attention to at the other homes she had been to. After a few weeks, she realized this couple was different. She learned never to let her guard down, even at ten years old, because she wasn't sure when she would be snatched from that home too.

"Did you wash your hands?" Marilyn asked, taking off the red and white apron she had on to cook. She was a Stepford mother and wife.

"Yes, ma'am," Promise replied, holding up her semi-wet hands.

"Good girl," Joseph said just as he walked into the kitchen before sitting down at the table.

Promise wasn't used to sitting down as a family to eat, because sometimes, she wasn't allowed to eat, and when she did, it was in her room alone. She loved moments like this. even if they weren't her real family.

"Joseph, could you bless the food?" Marilyn asked once she was seated.

"Let's bow our heads," Joseph said, putting his hands out palm up so that both Marilyn and Promise could take them.

That's another thing Promise wasn't used to—blessing the food and just praying in general.

"Dear heavenly father, we thank you for this day, and I come to you right now thanking you for allowing us to have another meal. I ask that the food be blessed, as well as the hands that prepared it. In your precious son's name, we all say amen," he prayed.

"Amen," Promise and Marilyn both said in unison.

"How was school today, Pumpkin?" Joseph asked before shoving a forkful of chicken alfredo into his mouth.

Promise loved that Joseph called her "pumpkin". It made

her think she was really their daughter and a part of the family, even if it was only for pretend.

"It was good. I received 100 percent on my spelling test. I was the only one in the class to do so," she said, not enthused at all. She wasn't used to anyone caring about how she did in school.

"Wow, sweetie! That is amazing," Marilyn said as she cut the lettuce in her side salad.

"Thank you," she said with a smile, but her voice still didn't sound enthused.

"Smiley, you should be a little more excited than that," Joseph said.

"Getting 100 percent is something to be proud of, and being the only one to do so is damn sure something to be proud of," he added.

"I am proud," she mumbled with a slight smile.

Promise was proud of herself. She just didn't know how to go about it.

"Then ya better say it a little more excitedly." He joked.

"I'm waiting," he said.

Promise's smile widened before she spoke. "I was the only one in my class to get 100 percent on my spelling test, and I am proud of myself." She beamed.

"And we're proud of you too." Marilyn smiled reaching over to touch Promise's hand.

Promise loved the Montgomerys, and she hoped to never leave, but she was almost positive she would eventually have to, sooner than later. She just had bad luck.

Chapter Seven

January 10th, 1997

Promise rode in the back seat of the 1997 Volvo as Joseph drove, and Marilyn sat quietly on the passenger side. It was eerily quiet. The radio wasn't even on like it normally was.

Seconds later, they pulled into a parking lot, and Joseph parked the car before climbing out, opening Marilyn's and Promise's doors.

"Are you ready to do this?" he asked Marilyn as he took her hands into his.

"As I'll ever be," she replied, looking down at Promise in her pretty blue and white plaid, ruffle dress with her laced socks rolled down and Mary Janes on her feet.

"Are you ready?" she asked just above a whisper, gazing in her eyes.

"Yes, ma'am," Promise answered.

Truth was, neither of them were ready, and they were all scared shitless. Ready or not, the time had come.

PROMISE SAT ON THE HARD, wooden bench, her mouth dry and hands sweaty. She was nervous.

"Case number RU8976390," the bailiff announced.

Joseph, Marilyn, and Promise all watched as their lawyer stood and gestured them to walk to the front. They all did as they were told.

"I am standing here on behalf of my clients," the lawyer started as she motioned to the trio, "with a petition to the court for an adoptive court rendered order for Miss Promise Love Lewis by Joseph and Marilyn Montgomery. The Montgomerys have previously petitioned the court, and I have noted documents that Jennifer Marie Lewis, Promise's biological mother, has terminated her rights as of December 11th, 1996," she spoke clearly.

The court fell quiet as the judge looked over all the necessary paperwork before removing his glasses and looking over at Promise.

"Young lady, could you come to the mic?" he politely asked.

At first Promise didn't move. It wasn't until Marilyn lightly nudged her that she moved.

"Could you state your full name?" he asked.

"Promise Love Lewis," she mumbled quietly into the mic, her voice shaky.

"How old are you, Promise?"

"Ten."

Once again, the room fell silent as the judge just simply stared at Promise.

"Would you like for your forever home to be with the Montgomerys?" he finally asked.

"Yes, sir." She smiled a little.

"Why is that?" he asked.

"Because," Promise started before clearing her throat as she shrugged, "they make me feel loved. I feel like I belong in their family. I haven't known them long, but from the first time I came into their lives, they have treated me like family," Promised said, briefly looking back at them both.

"Plus, I have my own room with a big bed," she said honestly, and everyone laughed lightly, but little did they know she meant this was the first time she had a nice room with an actual bed.

Once again, the courtroom fell silent as the judge looked down at the paperwork.

"Mr. and Mrs. Montgomery, please come forward," he said, and they did as they were told.

"Why do you want to adopt this beautiful little girl?"

Marilyn started. "She is an answered prayer. Promise completes our family. We couldn't imagine her not being in it," she simply said as they now stood next to Promise.

"When I look at Promise, I see a little girl who wants nothing more than someone to love her. She wants to be understood, but most importantly, she wants to be included. Promise is included in our family, and as my wife said, we couldn't imagine our life without her, and honestly, we don't want to."

Joseph wasn't a sentimental person, so he didn't even realize he was shedding tears until the lawyer handed him some Kleenex. He loved Promise.

"I hereby grant the legal adoption of Promise Love Lewis to Joseph and Marilyn Montgomery on the 10th day of January 1997." The judge smiled before bringing the gavel down on to the coaster-shaped wood.

Promise quickly turned to her now new parents with a smile and hugged them both tightly with tears flowing freely.

"Promise Montgomery." Promised beamed with tears in her eyes as she looked into her parents' eyes.

She was finally happy.

Eight

July 26th, 1999

"Hey, Daddy." Promise greeted her father when he stepped out of his car after pulling into the garage as she was practicing her ballet routine.

They had turned part of the garage into a mini ballet studio for Promise to practice in. She was dedicated to ballet. Promise was now twelve, in the sixth grade, and excelling at her private catholic school, Walsingham Academy.

"Hey, beautiful." He greeted before going to fetch the mail from the box.

"Extend that leg more, Promise," Marilyn coached as she watched Promise practice her arabesque.

Promise was the prima donna for the upcoming recital, and her mother wanted her to be perfect just like she once was when she danced.

"Yes, ma'am." Promise smiled doing as she was instructed.

"Good job."

Just as Promise was getting into the position to do the

attitude pose, she noticed her father walking back from the mailbox with worried lines on his forehead.

"Joseph, what's wrong?" Marilyn asked, noticing them as well.

"Daddy?" Promise questioned when she noticed a look in his eyes she had never witnessed—fear.

Joseph didn't respond to either of them.

Marilyn took the letter that Joseph was holding, which was obviously making him act the way he was. She quickly skimmed the letter.

"Oh no," she whispered, looking up at Joseph just before finally landing her eyes on Promise, who was now wearing a look of fear.

She had never seen either of her parents like this. Before Promise could ask what was wrong again, she heard her mother yell out the most horrific sound she had ever heard.

"She is ours! There is no way she can do this! She can't do this, can she?" Promise heard her mother yell out before dropping the letter, storming in the house, and her daddy quickly followed to console his wife.

Promise hadn't been this scared since first coming to live with her parents. Swallowing hard, Promise slowly bent down, picking up the paper her mother had dropped.

"No!" Promise cried out when she read her birth mother was back and trying to dispute the legal adoption of her.

Promise couldn't stop the tears that was coming fast, no matter how hard she batted her eyes.

"She can't do this," she whispered, shaking her head slowly and turning to walk into the house to follow her parents.

"Call Pamela. There is no way this is legal," Promise heard her mother cry, referring to the family lawyer, as she stood beside her father while he dialed a number.

"Oh, Promise," Marilyn said, noticing Promise standing in the doorway.

"Mommy," she whispered but never moved, "I don't want her to take me." Her voice was shaky and low.

Marilyn was hurting. Reading the letter did unknown things to her, but hearing her daughter's voice with so much hurt in it, along with seeing her sweet face looking the most hurt she had ever seen, snapped her back into motherhood.

"This is your home." She started as she quickly walked to Promise pulling her into a tight hug.

"No one is going to take you, even if I use every breath in my body to fight that," she spoke clearly as she pulled Promise away from her but still held her shoulders as she looked deeply in her teary, brown eyes.

"This is your home, Promise. We're your parents. No matter what, that will never change," Marilyn said in a reassuring tone before kissing her forehead gently.

"Do you understand that?"

Promise smiled. The tears continued falling as she nodded her head in agreeance. She had heard her mother. She hoped she was right, but she could only hope no bad would come from this. However, considering all the bad that had happened in her life, she didn't have her hopes too high.

———

"DEAR GOD, please don't let my birth mother come back and take me. I am happy where I am now. God, I promise if you don't let me leave here, I will never be disobedient at all. This is the first time in my life that I have ever been this happy, so please, please, God, let me stay right where I am. Please, God. In Jesus name, amen."

Joseph stood at Promise's door, watching her as she was on her knees leaned on her bed praying. He originally came to kiss her good night, but when he got to her door, he heard her praying, so he stopped and listened.

He watched as she pulled her pink and purple comforter back on her queen-sized bed before climbing in it. Joseph slowly backed away from the door. He now had tears of his own, so he couldn't face her. He knew he couldn't lose his baby girl, no matter who was coming to try and take her.

Promise belonged to him and his wife. This wouldn't be easy, but he would fight tooth and nail to keep her home where she belonged.

Chapter Nine

October 21st, 1999

Today was the day everyone had dreaded—court day. Thirteen-year-old Promise sat on the long, wooden bench between her parents as they waited for their case number to be called. Promise couldn't sleep one bit last night. She was terrified she would have to go back to Jennifer, and she didn't want that at all.

The door in the back of the court room creaked when it opened. Promise slowly turned around to see if it was Jennifer since she wasn't in the courtroom yet. It wasn't her. It was already past the time that court was supposed to start for them, but Jennifer hadn't made it, or she was present and Promise just forgot how she looked.

Slowly panning the courtroom, she tried to spot a familiar face, but by the time she scanned the entire room, she realized she didn't know anyone.

"Case number 9827657, Montgomery vs Jennifer Lewis," the bailiff said.

Promise, her parents, and their lawyer stood walking to the front. Promise's hands were sweaty, and she self-consciously rubbed them on her yellow and white floral dress before reaching over to her father, placing her small hands in his. He stepped into his role as her protector. Joseph gave Promise a reassuring smile as he lightly squeezed her hand. Beside the four of them, no one else stepped forward, and the bailiff realized it.

"Case number 9827657, Montgomery vs Jennifer Lewis," he called out again.

The big door in the back of the room creaked. Everyone turned except Promise. She couldn't bring herself to turn around. She just knew it was Jennifer walking in.

"My name is Jake Hudson," Promise heard. Looking beside her, she noticed an older white man with salt and pepper hair and far too many wrinkles on his overly tanned face. Jennifer was not in sight.

"I am here on behalf of Jennifer Lewis. I am her lawyer," he added.

"Where is Ms. Lewis?" the judge asked, peering over at Jake through his big, framed spectacles.

"I have a written letter that has a witness signature and has been notarized by a notary from Ms. Lewis stating that she is no longer interested in fighting for the custody of Promise Love Lewis." His tone was monotone, but Promise could hear sadness in it.

"Excuse me, Promise Love Montgomery." He corrected himself.

"Hand me that." The judge sighed.

Promise and her parents watched quietly as the judge read the letter, and stress lines formed on his dark-chocolate skin.

"Is Ms. Lewis present today in the courtroom?" he asked no one in particular without looking up from the letter.

"She is not," Jake mumbled.

The judge slowly removed his glasses before pinching the bridge of his pointy nose while raising his eyes to look in the direction of Promise and her parents.

"Promise, Mr. and Mrs. Montgomery, I want to apologize for causing chaos in your life today." He apologized before looking right at Promise.

"Promise, are you happy where you are with the Montgomery family?"

"Yes, sir." Her voice was low and shaky, and she was nervous.

The judge looked down at the paper before saying a few things to Jake, who jotted some things down. Then he said something to Promise's parents that she really didn't understand. Just as he hit his gavel, Marilyn picked Promise up and twirled her around before placing her firmly on her feet.

"You never have to worry about someone trying to take you from us ever again. You're right where you belong." She beamed with tears in her eyes.

Promise didn't fully understand what the judge had said, but after hearing what her mother said, she got the gist of what he had said.

"I love you."

"I love you too, Mommy," Promise replied as they both were pulled into a tight hug by Joseph.

PROMISE WAS ecstatic that she had a forever home with her parents, but she would be lying if she didn't say just a piece of her was hurt that her birth mother didn't show up in court today. She had it all—her own room with a bathroom, attended a top-rated private school, was spoiled without question, in every sport activity one could think of, and loved wholeheartedly by both Joseph and Marilyn, yet she still longed for her birth mother's love. She didn't understand how a person couldn't want their own flesh and blood.

"Hey, Promise, ready for game night?" Marilyn asked from the doorway as she held up a stack of board games.

"Yes, ma'am," was her simple reply as she stood from her bed.

Promise had questions but didn't need the answers, because all the love she needed came right from where she needed it most—Marilyn and Joseph.

Ten

June 2003

"I really can't believe we graduate in a week," Promise's best friend, Nicole, said as they sat on the edge of the underground pool in Promise's backyard.

Nicole and Promise had been best friends since Promise started going to Walsingham Academy years ago. She was the first one to talk to Promise. The pair were night and day. Nicole was a white, skinny, blonde-haired, blue-eyed cheerleader with the most country accent for someone who lived in Virginia that anyone has ever heard. Promise was black and thick with long, black hair and absolutely hated cheerleading.

"I know."

"Your speech all prepared?" Nicole's voice didn't match her tiny frame. Her voice was very husky like a woman in her forties that smoked two packs of Marlboro cigarettes a day.

Promise was only sixteen years old. She was graduating a

year earlier than she was supposed to and at the top of her class at that because she was so smart. Pulling her oversized shades down on her nose to peer at Nicole, she playfully rolled her eyes.

"You want the truth?" She laughed.

"I have started that thing and stopped it so many times it's not even funny. It's honestly like I can't find the right angle," she admitted.

"Don't stress it. Even if you don't come up with a written speech beforehand, I know you. Once you get to the podium, the right words will come out." Nicole encouraged Promise.

"Thank you."

"I am just ready to be off to college away from my strict ass parents."

Nicole's parents were the strictest of the strict. Besides Promise, she wasn't allowed to spend the night at anyone else's home. Even that took years to happen.

Promise placed her long hair that flowed down her back into a messy bun before sliding down into the warm water, which the sun beamed freely on.

"You're just worried about being alone with Mario," she teased, referring to Nicole's on-and-off-again high-school sweetheart.

"I mean..." she dragged as she, too, slid down in the water.

"It's a plus that he is attending the same school I am, but he's really not the reason." She giggled.

"You have the perfect set of parents, the perfect life, everything." The hint of jealousy was evident in her voice. "You have always had the best life."

Nicole knew all about Promise's past and how she came to the Montgomerys, but comments like the one she just made had Promise thinking she sometimes forgot. Promise couldn't help but slightly roll her eyes.

"Your parents love you, and your life has never been horrible."

"Oh my gosh, Promise. You know I wasn't implying the little shit I experienced in my life was anywhere near comparable to yours."

Promise hated that people saw her life now and where she was today and assumed her life had always been perfect. No, she didn't want to live in the past, but she wanted people to know she wasn't always loved and spoiled like she had become accustomed to.

"I know you didn't, crazy." She laughed as she playfully splashed her best friend.

Nicole was a rich, spoiled kid whose parents didn't play when it came to her, so them being super overprotective of her came off as more than it really was. Nicole playfully splashed Promise back before the smile she wore slowly turned into a frown.

"What?" Promise's smile never faded.

"I am happy to be going off to college and stuff, but it sucks that we will literally be on opposite sides of the world from each other, and I don't even know how that will work when we have spent every day together since we met when we were ten years old."

Nicole had been accepted to Arizona State University, where Promise had been accepted to multiple schools but was choosing to attend the University of Pennsylvania.

"Yeah. It's going to suck, but you're my best friend, so we will talk daily. Plus, it's not forever."

Promise's answer may have sounded like she didn't care, and though she really did, she was used to leaving people she was close with or them leaving her. She had become numb to the entire process.

"True," Nicole casually said. She knew Promise well

enough to know how she was feeling, so she wasn't about to press it.

"So about this speech…" She quickly changed the subject.

"It'll get done," Promise simply replied before going under the water and coming back up just as quickly as she went down.

Nicole knew she didn't want to talk about that either, so she wasn't going to hound her about it.

PROMISE SAT HER DESK, balling up the tenth piece of paper. She was trying to write her speech for graduation, but every time she was getting somewhere, it went way left.

Knock, knock!

"Come in," Promise mumbled just as she turned away from her desk, and in walked her daddy.

"Hey, Smiley. What's up?"

Promise couldn't help but smile at the nickname. He had given her that nickname when she came to them as a foster child; it was either that or Pumpkin. He didn't use it often.

"Hey, Daddy." She continued smiling. "I am trying to write this speech for graduation, but I am not getting anywhere."

"Let me see," he said, sitting on her bed across from her, reaching his hand out.

She handed him the most recent balled-up paper. Promise watched him intently. It was hard to tell what he was thinking since his facial expression never changed.

"So?" She bit her bottom lip nervously. "What do you think?"

"You're smart, always have been. This speech is something you want to be memorable for you and all the other students. Take a deep breath, relax, and just write."

"Daddy, I have been doing that, and I am stuck," she whined.

Standing to his feet, he handed Promise the crinkled-up paper back.

"Dig deep, and search within. You've got this." He encouraged her before kissing her forehead.

"Don't be afraid to speak your truths," he added before walking out of the room.

Promise heard her father, even replayed Nicole's words in her head, but she was still stuck.

"Ugh!" She tossed her head back, looking to the ceiling, silently praying she would get what she needed soon because graduation was approaching.

Chapter Eleven

June 15th, 2003

"And now we will hear a few words from the class of 2003's valedictorian, Promise Montgomery," Promise heard the principal say.

When the applause started, she stood to her feet, wiping her sweating hand on her silk purple gown. She had thought about this more times than she could count, even talked about it, but the moment was now here. It was now or never.

"Good afternoon." She greeted the audience, adjusting her robe, though it wasn't out of place.

Promise looked down at the speech she had spent forever writing before looking up and out into the stadium filled with people waiting on her to start. Closing her eyes tightly trying to shake her nerves, she slowly opened them, and when she did, they landed on her parents, who both wore smiles.

"I had this entire speech written out, but now that I am standing up here, I would rather freestyle this." She smiled. "I hope y'all don't mind?" She sighed. Promise begin speaking without waiting for a response from the crowd.

"Keep going, my friends." She started, and it didn't make sense.

"Most of my peers here today know that when I was just seven years old, my biological mother abandoned me at a local police station. I didn't understand why my own mother would leave," she said, pausing.

"Take your time, love," she heard Nicole say, and when she looked her way, she smiled at Promise reassuringly.

"It hurt growing up knowing I wasn't enough for her." Her voice began to crack, so she stopped, not wanting to cry.

"Knowing that I wasn't enough hurt, and for a while, it stopped me from excelling in life. I questioned God on many occasions, but even while questioning him, I always prayed my mother would come back and get me." She paused as she locked eyes with her parents.

"When I was ten years old, God answered my prayers. Only thing was, my birth mother didn't come back. Instead, he sent me my *real parents*," she said, emphasizing real parents.

"You see, we may not have the same blood running through our veins, but from day one, they've been my real parents. I said all of that to say my parents made me into the person I am today. I have had many struggles, but look at me, a little girl from downtown Newport News that was abandoned like a piece of trash. I have been accepted to twenty-seven schools, with full scholarships to twenty-one of them. My past did not define me," she said with a smile as the tears she once tried to fight fell freely, and everyone stood clapping and cheering.

"Keep going, my friends. No matter what is thrown your way, no matter how hard it may seem, no matter how many times you're denied, one time will matter. No matter what you do, keep going."

Promise ended her speech before stepping down from the podium. The people who filled the stadium were on their feet clapping and cheering. Her speech *would* be memorable.

"I AM SO PROUD OF YOU!" Joseph beamed as he lifted Promise from her feet, hugging her.

"Thank you, Daddy."

"I love you so much," Marilyn said once it was her turn to hug Promise.

"You have made us so proud, and I am so honored to be your mother," she said, her voice shaky and her lip quivering.

"Mommy," Promise whined as she batted her eyes, trying not to ruin her flawless makeup more than it already was from crying earlier.

"I love you too, Mommy," she was able to finally say.

Marilyn pulled Promise into a tight hug, never wanting to let her daughter go. Promise was the best thing that happened to her and Joseph, and they were the best thing that happened to her.

"I love you," she whispered in Promise's ear before kissing her cheek.

This was a beautiful moment.

Chapter
Twelve

May 10th, 2005

"I have to study for finals," Promise said in annoyance as she leaned her head away from her boyfriend, Tyriq, avoiding his puckered lips.

Promise was a junior at the University of Pennsylvania, where she was studying nursing. Promise and Tyriq had been dating on and off for a while now, and though Promise thought she was in love with Tyriq, he wasn't the best for her, and she knew it.

"You should be studying too," she added, pushing a stubborn curl behind her ear before sticking her pencil she had been writing with in her hair.

"Baby, I'm gonna study. Right now, I'm trying to slide inside you." His voice was raspy as he rubbed her thighs.

Promise had given her virginity to Tyriq about four months into their relationship. Though it was her choice to have sex, she hated that all he ever wanted to do was have sex.

Tyriq stood at an even six feet tall. He had a muscular build, light skin, dark-brown eyes, and a dick that had women hypnotized. At one point, he even had Promise gone, but lately, he was getting on her nerves more and more.

Promise sucked her teeth hard as she rolled her eyes even harder.

"Is that the only reason you wanted to come over?" Promise lived in a one-bedroom luxury apartment that her parents paid for each month.

"Nah. That ain't the only reason." He chuckled, sitting back on her bed that was near her desk.

"Good, because I ain't in the mood."

Tyriq huffed hard as he stepped back from Promise, looking at her pissed.

"Damn, Promise. You're my girlfriend. This holding out shit dead." It was clear he was pissed.

"Tyriq, what the hell do you want me to do?" she questioned while sucking her teeth.

"I want you to take care of my needs. Shit, I'm twenty-one. This shit has to be taken care of."

Tyriq was two years older than Promise and should have been about to graduate, but since he had been on academic probation and lost his football scholarship, he was only a junior like Promise.

Closing her eyes tightly, Promise slowly turned her pink computer chair around to fully face Tyriq.

"You got needs, huh?" She chuckled before pausing while biting her bottom lip.

Promise wasn't the least bit in the mood, but she knew if she didn't do something Tyriq would come with his same tired as line that someone else would take her spot.

"Hell yeah!" he fired back his voice low and raspy as he pulled Promise to him by her thighs while she still sat in the computer chair.

Tyriq slowly snaked his tongue along the outside of Promise ear before gently nibbling on her neck while she caressed his growing dick through his basketball shorts.

"Why you always playing hard to get, girl?" he asked just as he felt her petite hands pull on the band of his shorts before one slipped inside his boxers.

"I don't know what you are talking about." She flirted as she ran her tongue along her teeth.

"Yeah, a'ight."

In one swift motion, Tyriq slipped his hands under Promise's butt, lifting her onto him as he leaned back on her queen-sized bed.

"You know your ass be wanting this dick. Always playing hard to get and shit."

Promise only smiled. Truth was, she didn't want his dick. Tyriq put it down, well at least she thought so, but truth was, she didn't have anyone else to compare him to. Either way, she didn't want the dick, at least not all the time.

After a short kiss, Tyriq rolled over, causing Promise to now be on her back. He stood to his feet, pulling his shorts and boxers down at the same time.

"You gon' take ya clothes off?" he questioned.

Damn. Your ass don't put any kind of spice in shit, she thought as she sat up on her elbows, sliding out of her Victoria's Secret capri sweatpants before pushing her cotton, black panties over her hips and down her legs, kicking them on the floor.

She watched as he pulled his T-shirt over his head. *What guy takes his pants off before his shirt?* she thought just as he slipped the condom he had taken out of his pocket onto his curved dick.

Tyriq quickly entered Promise with no foreplay. Hell, he didn't even check to make sure she was wet. Just as quickly as he entered her, he started moving. The first few pumps were slow, but that didn't last long.

"Fuck, baby. Your pussy good as shit," he moaned.

Promise scrunched her face up as he pumped faster.

"Fuck. I'on wanna cum," he damn near moaned like a girl.

"I can't hold this shit in." He was breathless as he made a loud screeching sound and got a massive hump in his back.

One minute and seven seconds? Promise thought. She looked at the oversized clock on her wall as Tyriq rolled off of her. That was seven seconds longer than the last time.

"You okay?" she asked as she looked over at him with his chest rising and falling and beads of sweat on his forehead.

"Yeah, baby. Can you get me some water?" he asked.

Fuck no was what she wanted to say, but she didn't. Instead, she slid to the edge of the bed, grabbing her silk robe that was thrown over her ottoman before heading to get his water. Though Tyriq was the only person she ever had sex with, she was almost positive it was supposed to be longer than what he ever offered. She was damn sure supposed to feel some type of excitement from it.

"You leaving?" she asked in an amused tone.

"Yeah, baby. I gotta be to work in the morning."

"Well, here." She handed him the bottle of Dasani water, unable to mask her disappointment.

"Call ya later?" His statement came out as more of a question.

"Cool."

Promise leaned against the wall near the front door as she tried to avoid his kiss, but he knew that was coming, so he was quicker than her.

"I love you," he said just as he was at the door.

"Love you too," she mumbled just before closing the door behind him before his left foot was over the threshold.

"Ugh." Promise sighed heavily as she walked back to her bedroom.

She loved Tyriq but was confused about him and the relationship they had. After their sex, if that was what it should be called, she was even more confused.

"It just has to be more to this than what I am getting." Promise sighed, sitting back at her computer studying.

The good thing about Tyriq not lasting long was she hadn't missed anything from studying.

Chapter Thirteen

June 29th, 2005

"Oh my goodness, Lavell. You're hilarious." Promise laughed so hard her light-colored skin turned a deep red.

"Ah, you're making my cheeks hurt." She continued laughing as she reached her hands up, touching both her hot cheeks.

Promise and Lavell were sitting in one of the school's dining halls when Lavell started with the jokes as he always had, causing her to laugh nonstop. Promise and Lavell met in their anatomy and physiology class. It was clear that they both were feeling each other, but since Promise was with Tyriq and loved him, she never even looked at Lavell as anything more than a friend.

It was summer, but Promise wanted to graduate early, so she didn't take any breaks.

Lavell was laughing too, but his laugh slowly came to a

halt when he looked across the room and saw Tyriq headed their way.

"Ya man coming. I hope it ain't no bullshit today," he added just before Tyriq reached them. It was clear he didn't like Tyriq.

Promise sat without a word as Tyriq reached her. When he did, he grabbed her face and kissed her deeply as if he was proving a point. He'd never kissed her that way.

"'Sup, baby." He greeted, sitting beside her and draping his arm across her shoulders.

"Hey," Promise whispered.

Promise knew Tyriq was only being extra because of Lavell.

"'Sup, Lavell." He smirked, finally acknowledging him.

"'Sup, man," Lavell casually spoke back.

Lavell wasn't a punk, but he knew how to choose his battles. He always felt Tyriq was a bitch and not even worth his energy.

"Promise, I'ma head home. I'll call ya later." Lavell stood to his feet.

Promise was about to respond, but before she could, Tyriq spoke up. "Nah, fam. Don't call her later. She gon' be tied up." He chuckled.

"Promise, call me." Lavell ignored Tyriq.

"Nigga, didn't I say she was gonna be busy?"

Lavell wanted to fire back, but when he looked at Promise and saw the look on her face begging him not to, he just nodded his head and walked off.

"Seriously?" Promise questioned leaning back from Tyriq's grasp.

"Fuck you mean 'seriously'?"

"You came over here interrupting us talking and then had the nerve to be rude."

"You my motherfucking girl! Fuck him!" he hissed.

"I mean, what? Y'all fucking or something?" He raised his voice.

Promise sucked her teeth. She looked at Tyriq as if he had grown a second head.

"I mean, what is it? Nigga stay in your face, calling or texting your ass, and now he butt hurt 'cause I said you'll be tied up tonight, and you taking his side." He paused as if he was thinking of all he had just mentioned.

"Y'all fucking?" he asked with his head cocked to the side.

"You're crazy," Promise replied, standing to her feet, not wanting to be around him any longer.

Tyriq roughly grabbed her wrist, squeezing it. She tried to pull away, but he squeezed tighter.

"That don't answer the fucking question!"

"Let go." She tried turning her wrist from his grip, but he didn't budge.

"People are staring," she mumbled just as people who were walking by slowed their stride.

"Fuck you," he said through gritted teeth as he stood to his feet still holding her wrist.

"This shit ain't over," he hissed, roughly dropping her wrist, almost popping her shoulder out of the socket before storming off.

"Is everything okay?" a couple walking by that had seen and heard the commotion asked.

"Ye-Yeah, I'm fine," Promise stuttered as she rubbed her sore wrist while watching Tyriq storm out of the dining hall.

This was the first time Tyriq had actually put his hands on Promise, but it wasn't the first time he had verbally abused her and made a scene. She could tell his reaction was getting more violent each time he got pissed.

"Hey, Mommy," Promise answered her ringing phone, placing it on speaker as she sat on her love seat, tucking her feet under her butt.

"Hey, Princess," Marilyn said chipperly but stopped when she heard the sadness in her daughter's voice.

"What's wrong, sweat pea?" Her tone soothing and concerning.

"Nothing," she dryly said as tears stung her eyes.

Something was wrong, and she wanted to tell her mother, but she also knew she would say the same thing she said the other four times Promise vented about Tyriq, so she didn't even want to involve her this time.

"What are you up to?" Promise quickly changed the subject.

Marilyn didn't speak right away. She knew when her daughter was lying. She also could tell she was upset because of that no-good boy she called a boyfriend, but being the mother she was, she didn't speak on it.

"Are you still coming down for the fourth?"

"Yes, ma'am. I am going to come down on the first."

Ding!

Promise's phone went off indicating she had a text message.

Tyriq: Promise, I love you. I know I keep fucking up, but baby, you're mine. I know you don't want Lavell, or anyone else for that matter, but my head keep getting fucked up. I love you, girl.

"Promise?" Marilyn said a little louder when Promise hadn't responded.

"Ma'am? Sorry. I was reading something. What did you say?"

"I said are you coming alone?" Marilyn was hoping she was, but even if she wasn't, Marilyn would be happy to see her either way.

"I'm not sure, Mommy." Promise sighed just as she got another message.

Tyriq: *Can I come over?*

Tyriq: *Please?*

"Oh." She couldn't hide her disappointment. "Well, either way, your father and I can't wait to see you. It has been so long since we last saw you."

Though Promise had saw her parents when they came to visit last year for Christmas, she hadn't actually been home since Thanksgiving.

"I know. I miss both of you." Promise hadn't responded to neither of Tyriq's texts, so he continued texting.

Tyriq: *Please let me come over.*

"We miss you too. All of the family will be happy..." Marilyn started, but her words trailed off when she heard a knock at Promise's door. "Do you need to go?"

"Yes, Mommy. Let me call you back," she said because she knew it was Tyriq at her door since she hadn't answered his text. Plus, he had tried to call her, but she didn't click over.

"Okay. I love you."

"I love you too," Promise said before hanging up as she stood to her feet.

"Who is it?" she spoke softly as she stood near the door, already knowing who it was.

"Baby, it's me." Tyriq sounded pathetic from the opposite side of the door.

"Open the door." His voice was low as he begged.

Promise took a deep breath before unlocking and slowly opening her door.

"What?"

"Can I come in?"

Instead of speaking, Promise backed away, opening the door wider, and he stepped in. She closed the door but didn't turn around to look at him. It was crazy how since she was ten years old, she had been in a loving home, but for some reason, she felt like that nine-year-old girl being mistreated.

"Promise," Tyriq called out as he walked toward her before wrapping his arms around her waist, hugging her tightly from behind.

"I fucked up," he added, and that's when the tears fell from Promise's eyes.

Promise was strong, yet at this moment she was weak. Tyriq was horrible for her, but she couldn't walk away, even though she wanted to.

"Why do you keep doing this?" she questioned as she turned around.

"Look at my wrist!" she added with tears as she held up her bruised wrist that had his handprint indented on it.

"Baby." Tyriq sounded pathetic. "I fucked up."

"Seriously?"

"I fucked up," he repeated.

He won't just admit he is wrong and apologize, Promise thought, looking up into his dark-brown eyes.

"Okay." She shrugged.

At this point, she was used to Tyriq fucking up, not apologizing, and coming back like it was all good. The only difference about before was he had never put his hands on her. She was at the end of the road with him.

Kissing her deeply, Tyriq didn't pull back until he had won her back or at least he thought.

"We good?" he asked.

"Yeah," was her simple reply.

Truth was, they weren't good. She just had to let go with her heart, so she could easily walk away, and that time was coming faster than not.

Chapter
Fourteen

July 5ᵗʰ, 2005

"Why'd you ask that, Daddy?" Promise asked as she sat on the edge of the pool at her parents' house, and her dad sat in the lounge chair next to her mother.

Joseph had just asked Promise how she was feeling lately.

Joseph cocked his head to the side, looking at his daughter as if he was saying *you already know why I'm looking this way.*

"One, baby girl, I didn't miss that your *little* boyfriend didn't come with you this time." He started putting an emphasis on little.

"Two, you haven't been acting like yourself. Three, I wasn't eavesdropping, but I heard you crying last night."

Promise was almost embarrassed because he was right; something was wrong. Tyriq didn't come because they had an argument. She wasn't herself lately because so much of

67

her time had been consumed with dealing with Tyriq's bullshit.

Yes, she was crying last night. She had come so far in life, yet she was settling for something she didn't have to accept.

"Daddy, I am fine." She lied with a fake smile plastered on her beautiful face.

"Smiley?" he called out, encouraging her to talk. He called her Smiley, though he hadn't seen her smile lately.

"Daddy, I am okay." She was trying more so to convince herself than him.

"I'm okay," she repeated.

Promise never lied to her parents, but she knew she couldn't tell her father the truth. She was daddy's little girl, and she knew if she told the truth he would go ape shit, so she had to lie for the first time.

"Okay," he replied, not giving it a second thought, and though he was leaving it alone, Promise knew this wasn't the end of it.

———

PROMISE: First off, I want you to know this is one of the hardest things I have ever done, and as much as I love you, I have to do this for me. We aren't good for each other. It's best we break up and go our separate ways before either of us gets hurt. I need to find out who I am because along the way, I have forgotten. Please understand that I truly love you, but I am doing this for me. We're done, Tyriq.

Promise sat on the side of her bed rereading the message she was about to send to Tyriq. She had typed it about five minutes ago but hadn't gotten the courage to send it.

"Now or never," she said out loud as she pressed the send button while closing her eyes tightly.

Knock, knock! Promise heard, startling her little bit.

"Come in." Her voice was jumpy.

"Did I scare you?" Joseph asked once he stepped into the room.

"A little, but I'm fine."

"Okay. I was just checking on you and wanted to say good night." He kissed her forehead before doubling back out the room.

"Daddy," she called out after him just as he was about to close the door.

He stepped back just looking at his daughter not saying a word.

"Can I talk to you?" Nervousness was evident in her voice.

"What's on your mind, baby girl?" he questioned, sitting next to her.

Promise took a deep breath as she held her head down before lifting it and looking into her father's awaiting eyes.

"Daddy, I think I'm in an abusive relationship," she finally admitted with tears in her eyes.

It took everything in Joseph not to blow up at hearing his daughter was being abused. He could tell she didn't need that right now.

"What do you mean you're in an abusive relationship?" was all he managed to get out since he was biting the hell out of his tongue.

"At first, Daddy, it was only verbal, but a few days ago he grabbed my wrist, leaving bruises," she admitted, holding out her wrist that she had hid well with makeup that matched her skin perfectly.

Joseph pinched the bridge of his nose. He had seen the bruises, but when his daughter said she was fine, he was half hoping they came from a bracelet being too tight, though he knew that wasn't the case.

"He did that to you?" He pointed.

"Daddy, I don't want you to get angry. I want some honest nonbiased advice," she spoke softly. "But yes Tyriq did this to me."

He heard her loud and clear, but seriously, how could he not be angry when someone hurt his baby girl?

"Promise," he called her name firmly, and Promise knew he was pissed. He never called her Promise.

"You're a beautiful young lady. Not only are you beautiful, but you're my daughter." He paused for a second because he was trying to calm down.

"You're not a punching bag. No one, and I mean no one, should ever put their hands on you, no matter what. And a man, well, someone who calls themselves a man, shouldn't dare put their damn hands on you," he said firmly.

"Daddy," she whined.

"Daddy nothing. Your mother and I raised you right. Don't let some fuck boy come in and ruin everything we have instilled in you." He leaned in, kissing the top of Promise's head before standing to his feet.

"Know your worth, Promise." His voice was low and soothing.

"I love you, baby girl." He had to leave before his anger showed more than it already was.

"I love you too, Daddy," she whispered as she watched him walk out of the room.

Promise knew her father's words were short because he was angry, and she understood why. Also, though he didn't say many words, he put a lot into perspective for her. She knew things had to change, and yesterday.

Before going to sleep, Promise checked her phone, hoping for a response from Tyriq, but to her surprise, there was nothing.

"Yup it's time for a change," she said with sadness and relief at the same time.

Chapter Fifteen

July 8th, 2005

Boom! Boom! Boom! Boom!

"What the hell?" Promise was startled when she heard the loud knocking on her front door. She had been back from Virginia only a few hours.

Looking through her peephole, she spotted Tyriq standing on the other side of her door with his hoodie thrown over his head.

"Tyriq, what the hel—" Promise started as she snatched open her front door, but her words were caught short when Tyriq stepped inside, wrapping his hands tightly around her small neck.

"You think I'm gonna fucking let you end shit with me?" he hissed as he tightened his grip around her neck while slamming her door with his foot.

Promise was clawing at his face, and though her nails were piercing his face, it didn't cause him to loosen his grip.

"You gon' fucking end this shit with me?" he shouted, finally letting her go.

Promise lay on the floor panting, trying to catch her breath as she grabbed at her chest.

"Answer me!" He kneeled beside her grabbing her long hair and wrapping it tightly in his fist.

Promise didn't answer fast enough, or maybe she even blinked wrong. Whatever the reason, Tyriq continued grabbing her hair and punched her in the nose with his free hand.

"Ahhh!" Promise cried in pain as blood dripped from her nose.

Just as Promise was about to say something, she saw the bottom of Tyriq's black Air Force Ones coming toward her face before connecting with it.

"Please," she begged just as he lifted it, bringing it down to her face again.

"I'm not going to end us," she cried as she tasted her blood while it dripped from her nose along with her salty tears that fell quickly.

"Don't fucking lie to me!" Tyriq roared, releasing her hair but not before punching her, causing her head to jolt back and collide with her fresh white walls.

In that moment, Promise knew she had to fight because even after saying she wasn't going to end them, he was still hurting her. There was a split second that Tyriq had blinked too long, and that gave Promise the opportunity to use all of her force to kick Tyriq in his groin.

"You stupid bitch!" he yelled out as he grabbed his dick.

Promise tried to make a run for it. All she needed to do was make it to her room where her cell phone was to call the police, and she would be fine. Just as she reached her room, she tried closing the door, but Tyriq was fast on her heels. She was able to grab her cell phone before he grabbed her hair, bringing her to the floor and dragging her back to the living room as she kicked and screamed.

Crack!

Promise's jaw cracked when Tyriq punched her, causing her to fall back on the floor. She used that moment to dial 911 on her phone, though Tyriq quickly kicked it out her hand. However, the call never disconnected.

"Help me!" she cried, her voice almost hoarse from the crying she had been doing.

"Please!" she begged.

"Nah, bitch! Ain't no helping you!"

He sounded wicked and possessed as he brought his knee up under her chin, causing her head to jerk back. It landed on the corner of the coffee table, knocking her out cold. Tyriq stood over top of her. His chest rising and falling quickly before kicking her roughly in the ribs, but she didn't move. She was out.

"Pennsylvania Police Department," Tyriq heard, which caused him to freeze in his tracks.

"Hands above your head, now!" the officer shouted, but Tyriq continued with his back toward him.

"Put your fucking hands up!" the officer demanded.

Tyriq knew he couldn't get away, so he complied as he stared down at Promise while she was rendered aid. He wasn't sure if he killed her, but as he was escorted out of her apartment, he was already regretting his decision to come to her house.

Sixteen

June 10th, 2008

Beep. Shh. Beep. Shhh, were the constant sounds Marilyn and Joseph heard from the heart machine and breathing machine as they sat at Promise's bedside. Promise was brought into the hospital of the University of Pennsylvania two days ago to the intensive care unit.

When Promise arrived, she had two black eyes—one of which were dislocated from its socket—along with a broken nose and jaw, two cracked ribs, numerous bruises, and her hair pulled directly from her scalp. Her parents almost didn't recognize her when they made it to the hospital.

Promise was expected to make it. Of course, she'd have a long road to recovery. Since she was beaten up so badly, they had her on morphine, so she slept ninety-eight percent of the time. She was in critical yet stable condition.

"Good morning." The friendly nurse that the Montgomerys had grown quite fond of greeted when she walked into the room after knocking.

"Good morning," they said in unison as they watched her wash her hands before checking things on Promise's machine.

"So Dr. Newkirk put in an order to lower Promise's morphine and discard the breathing machine. As of right now, he just wants her on a low dose of morphine and the heart monitor and of course to watch her normal vital sign readings."

"Does that mean she will get to come home soon?" Marilyn asked excitedly as she rubbed Promise's hand.

"Well, we can't get ahead of ourselves. First, we need to wean her off of the medicine and then remove the breathing machine and see how she reacts to that. Then we would need to get her eating properly, and lastly, we will have her seen by the ophthalmologist. So the long answer, yes. Eventually, she will go home, but as of right now, we're taking small steps into getting her in the right direction." She informed them as she started changing the numbers on the machine that was administering the morphine.

"So once the morphine starts wearing down a bit, she will wake up disoriented. She may not speak right away, but no worries, that is all normal," she added.

"Give Promise an hour or two, and let her body do what it is supposed to do," she said with a smile before washing her hands and leaving the same way she entered.

"What if she doesn't do what she's supposed to do?" Marilyn asked, her voice shaky as she looked down at her beautiful daughter looking unrecognizable as she stroked her natural, springy curls.

"She's a fighter, honey. She will be fine." Joseph tried to reassure his wife, though he wasn't even confident in the words he had just spoken. He could only pray.

MARILYN HAD her head down holding tightly onto Promise's hand as Joseph stared out the huge window looking out into the city. Promise began slowly opening her eyes and moving her hands, causing Marilyn to lift her head and look at her daughter. Promise tried to move but realized the pain was so much, so she relaxed as tears begin to fall down the sides of her custard-colored skin.

"Mommy," she whined, slowly licking her dry, cracked lips.

Joseph walked to his daughter's bedside and grabbed her other hand.

"Daddy," she whined, looking at him.

Promise closed her eyes tightly as the tears continued to fall.

"I'm-I'm so sorry," she stuttered as she looked back and forth between her parents.

"I'm sorry," she repeated.

"Shhh, baby girl," Joseph said, kissing her forehead. "You have nothing to be sorry for, this isn't your fault." He soothed.

Promise heard him loud and clear that it wasn't her fault, but to her, it was her fault. Had she left Tyriq months ago when he first started showing signs of the rage he displayed the other night, she wouldn't be lying in a hospital bed right now.

It is my fault, she thought as she lay there with tears falling slowly.

Chapter
Seventeen

June 12th, 2008

"Promise, there are two detectives here to speak with you, but I explained to them that if you were not ready, then they would have to come back another time," Dr. Newkirk spoke as he sat on the rolling stool. "Would you like to talk to them now, or have them come back?"

Promise was a long way from being her normal self, but she was no longer connected to any machines. She was eating soft foods and doing well in therapy.

"I can talk to them," she mumbled.

Promise knew this day would come. Since she wanted to quickly get it over with, she felt like now was the best time to do it.

"Alright…" he dragged. He personally felt she wasn't ready, but he couldn't stop her.

"Nurse Lola and I will be right outside if you need us." His tone was reassuring so she would know she wasn't alone.

"Okay." She barely looked his way as he walked out of her room, and seconds later, two plain clothes officers with badges dangling from their necks and 9 mm guns strapped to their thighs walked in.

"Good morning, Ms. Montgomery. My name is Detective Yarbury, and my partner is Detective Cabello," the taller of the two officers spoke first.

"We're here to get some information on the attack that you endured," he added, not waiting for Promise to reply to him saying good morning. "Are you able to answer some questions?"

"Yes," Promise answered, already wishing she had said she wasn't ready for this since the officers were staring at her as if she was a criminal.

Detective Yarbury nodded to Detective Cabello, and he pulled out a notepad while moving closer to Promise.

"As Detective Yarbury stated, I am Detective Cabello." He started, and Promise could tell he was the nicer of the two.

"First off, I do want to apologize for what has happened to you. I also want to make you aware that we're here to take your statement from everything that happened that night. If at any time during the interview it becomes overwhelming, let me know and we can stop," he stated.

"Okay." She watched as he pulled out a black tape recorder.

"I am going to press record on this recorder and begin asking questions. This recorder is for your safety as well as mine. Would you like to continue?"

"Yes, sir," she whispered.

"We will now begin," Detective Cabello said, pressing record on the tape recorder.

"Ma'am, could you please state your name and date of birth?" he asked, sounding like a robot. She could tell he did this on a daily basis.

"Promise Love Montgomery." Her voice was barely audible. "August 18th, 1986."

"Ma'am, could you speak up?" Detective Yarbury said, sounding more demanding than asking a question.

"Promise Love Montgomery." It was clear she was already irritated.

"Ms. Montgomery, could you tell us what happened on the night of July 8th, 2008? Try to be as detailed as possible."

Promise took a deep breath as she closed her eyes before opening them.

"I was sitting at home watching TV when I heard a few loud knocks at my door, so I opened it, and that—" Her words were cut off by Detective Yarbury.

"You opened your door without asking who it was?" he asked in an unbelieving tone.

"I looked through the peephole and noticed it was my boyfriend." She stopped. "Well, recently ex-boyfriend Tyriq, so I opened the door."

"And then what took place?" Detective Cabello asked as both detectives jotted down things.

"Once the door was open, he immediately began choking me. I tried prying his hands from my neck, but he was much stronger than me." Her voice began to crack as she felt the tears about to come.

"He was shouting a lot of different things but mainly calling me a bitch and things. Before I knew it, he punched me a few times." She paused wiping her tears.

"I was able to break free after kicking him in his private. When I broke free, I grabbed my phone, calling 911, but once he grabbed me, hitting me again, I lost control of my phone." She stopped.

"Anything else?" Detective Yarbury asked with no remorse in his voice.

"I am so sorry that happened to you. Is there anything

you would like to add?" Detective Cabello quickly asked because he hated the way his partner was handling Promise.

"I don't remember much after grabbing my phone since he continued hitting me, causing me to slam my head. Eventually, I blacked out," she cried while only focusing on Detective Cabello.

"Ms. Montgomery, I can't imagine what you went through, but I hope you can accept my sincerest apology. I want to also say how courageous you were by calling the police. Your doing so allowed our dispatcher to hear the commotion and get officers to you." He smiled, and she smiled back at him.

"Tyriq Smith is in custody and is being held without bond. He has been charged with attempted murder and two counts of felony assault along with trespassing. I can assure you that with your cooperation, he will not be released."

Promise never wanted Tyriq to go to jail, but she also didn't expect to be laying in a hospital bed bruised, broken, and hurt, being questioned by two detectives for the pain that he caused.

"Is there anything else you would like to add?"

"No, sir."

Promise watched as he pressed stop on the recorder while grabbing her some Kleenex that sat on the bedside table.

"If at any time you remember something else or just would like to know information on the case, you can reach me at any one of these numbers," he said, handing out the Kleenex and a business card.

"Okay, and thank you." She sniffled.

"Have a good day." Detective Yarbury was already halfway out of the door.

"You too," she said with a smile as she watched him walk out.

"Lord, help me," she cried, reaching up, touching her swollen bruised cheek.

She was recovering well physically, but she knew that it would take a while before she recovered mentally.

Chapter
Eighteen

It had been almost a year since Tyriq attacked Promise in her home, and the day had finally come where she would face him one last time; it was verdict day. It took Promise months to get back to her normal self, and her hair had grown back thicker than before. It was taking her a lot longer to heal the emotional wounds.

"Are you okay?" Promise's lawyer asked her as they, along with Promise's parents, climbed the many stairs that led inside the courthouse.

"Yes, ma'am," she replied just as they reached the top stair and she paused briefly.

"I am just glad this about to be over." She sighed.

This was the fourth time being in this courtroom. The first three times were for Tyriq's trial where she had to testify, but that was almost five months ago.

"Alright, let's do it," she said, placing one foot in front of the other.

Entering the courtroom where the sentencing would take place, Promise looked around the room and realized how cold it looked paired badly with it actually being cold in the room. The room only housed four long, wooden benches—two on each side—a small, narrow walkway that led to the front. On one side was the plaintiff's side, which had a small table and three steel chairs, and the same for the defendant's side.

The biggest areas of the courtroom were where the twelve jurors would sit and the area directly in the middle of the courtroom where the judge sat.

"It's going to be okay, baby," Joseph whispered in Promise's ear as he intertwined his fingers with hers since he was already holding Marilyn's hand.

Promise, her lawyer, and Joseph sat at the three chairs on the plaintiff's side. Marilyn sat on the first row directly behind them.

"All rise!" they heard the bailiff say just as they sat down before they all stood to their feet.

"The division of criminal court of Pennsylvania is now in session. The honorable Judge Mack presiding."

The bailiff rambled off a few other things, but Promise wasn't listening, because she was nervous as hell. She was so zoned out she didn't even hear when he said everyone could be seated. It wasn't until her lawyer tapped her that she checked back in.

"Bring in the defendant," the judge said, looking over his thin, speckled glasses.

Seconds later, a side door opened, and out walked Tyriq. *Oh my gosh,* Promise thought, looking over at him.

Tyriq had shackles on his feet, which had a long chain that connected to the cuffs that were around his wrists. He shuffled his way into the courtroom. Tyriq held his head down as he walked to his seat, and once he reached it, he looked over at Promise, and a chill ran up her spine as they locked eyes.

I can't believe I was once in a relationship with him, and thought I loved him, she thought, quickly averting her eyes.

"Has the jury reached a verdict?" the judge questioned.

"We have," once of the jurors answered, holding out a folded piece of paper, which the bailiff took.

The judge looked down at the paper before looking over at the jurors.

"I am going to ask a question, and once I call on a juror, you either say yes or no," he stated.

"Was this verdict your choice without being forced?" he asked, and one by one each juror said yes.

"Juror number five, could you please read the verdict."

Juror number five stood.

"Your Honor, the members of this jury find the defendant, Tyriq Sean Smith, guilty on all charges," she said, and Promise gasped the second she heard it.

Promise looked over at Tyriq and realized he hadn't even flinched when the guilty verdict was read. He had no remorse.

"Members of the jury, this court dismisses you, and thank you for the job well done," the judge said, and all twelve members of the jury stood to their feet.

"Mr. Smith, I hereby sentence you to twenty-five years to life without the possibility of parole." The judge handed down the sentence once the jury was out of the courtroom.

Tears slid down Promise's light-colored cheeks. She was happy yet sad at the same time. Though justice had been served, she knew she could never get back the time she had lost.

Chapter
Nineteen

July 19th, 2011
Two years later...

Time was critical, and Promise knew every second counted. She knew her chances were slim, but she refused to allow the eight-year-old girl who had come into the ER with a gunshot wound to the chest to die.

"Promise, call it," the doctor in the room said just as he was removing his sterile blue suit.

About three other doctors and a handful of nurses stood off to the side, also removing their gear.

"No!" she shouted, out of breath as she continued chest compressions.

"Promise, call it!" he retorted.

The doctor was in charge, but since Promise was the one who started the compressions, she was the one who would declare the time of death. She refused.

"Call it!" His tone now demanding.

Promise looked at the doctor with a mean glare in her

eyes, but she never slowed her motions. She wasn't giving up. Just as she was about to say she wasn't stopping, she heard the heart machine begin to slowly beep, no longer sounding the long beep.

"I said I wasn't giving up," she said, firmly looking at the doctor, who now wore a shocked, dumbfounded look.

"Dr. Simple, take over from here. Promise, I want to speak to you privately," he said through clenched teeth before walking out other trauma room.

"Good job," Promise heard a small whisper from the older nurse say just as she was preparing to walk out the room. She simply smiled and nodded in response.

"Come in," Promise heard a deep voice say after she knocked on the door.

Holding her head high, Promise slowly pushed the office door open before walking in.

"Have a seat." His tone still demanding.

Promise almost wanted to ask who the hell he thought he was talking to, but instead, she kept her mouth closed and sat down as she was told.

"My name is Dr. Hassan Davis, and that ER you just defied me in is *my* ER."

Promise didn't know Hassan's name since this was the first time she had worked with him, and when they were introduced things were already intense, so she didn't catch his name.

"With all due respect, Dr. Davis," she drawled, "you may be the head doctor in the ER, but I am the head nurse. Tonight, I made a choice and a damn good one might I add. You told me call time of death on a patient that I was able to save, and had I not, that little girl would not be alive right now." Promise was proud of the decision not to listen to Dr. Hassan, and if she had to do it again, she would.

Dr. Davis sat behind his desk, staring back at Promise.

His shoulder length locs were pulled back in a low ponytail, and his brown skin was a perfect shade of extra-toasty bread. He had a full sleeve of tattoos, and he had that rugged look.

Promise could tell by the way his chiseled jawline tightened that he didn't like her response.

"You may have saved this one, but what if you ignored my call like you did, and you didn't have the same outcome?" he questioned, leaning onto his desk, staring intently at Promise.

It was almost comical to Promise how he was acting. She wasn't sure if he was mad because she defied him in front of others, or because she made a call that had a better outcome than what he thought. Either way, it was almost laughable, but she kept her poker face on.

"Again, Dr. Davis," she said his name clearly as she, too, sat up in her seat, "the other outcome should not matter at this moment. I saved a life. We work in a trauma ER, and you know, just as well as I know, things get hectic, but our number-one goal is to keep people alive so they can live another day and see their families. We had an eight-year-old girl arrive, who had already coded, but I was able to resuscitate her. I don't understand why you aren't praising me," she quipped with sass but remained as polite as possible.

"I saved the life of a beautiful, eight-year-old girl, and we can proudly tell her parents she will be okay, rather than apologizing saying she didn't make it," she added.

He knew Promise was right, and he was actually happy about the outcome. He just needed her to understand that he was the doctor, and she was the nurse, and the calls he made trumped hers, even if they weren't always the best.

"Ms. Montgomery is it?" he questioned with a smirk, which let Promise know he knew that was her name.

"It's Promise."

"Sorry, Promise. Thank you for saving a life." He half-ass complimented.

"But from now on, when you're in the ER with me and I make a call, you follow what I say," he commanded.

There was so much Promise wanted and could have said, but she learned through life that every action didn't need a reaction. Not only that, but she could tell he wasn't going to really be grateful for the choice she made.

"Duly noted." She rolled her eyes.

"Will that be all?" she asked, standing to her feet, pretty much telling him that would be all.

"For now."

"Enjoy the rest of your night, Dr. Davis," she sarcastically said before walking out the office.

Twenty

July 21st, 2011

Hassan stood off the side, leaning on the nurse's station, watching Promise go over the shift change checklist with the charge nurse for day shift. He had seen Promise on a few occasions since their first encounter, and if he was honest with himself, he was heavily attracted to her. He didn't realize how hard he was staring until Promise looked up from the iPad with a smile, which caused him to quickly look away.

Promise started walking his way. He tried to act like he was looking at his computer screen. He wasn't doing a good job hiding.

"Good evening, Dr. Davis," Promise spoke in a smart-aleck tone when she reached him.

Hassan saw her walking his way, even watched her mouth move, but he didn't hear a word she said, because he was stuck in a trance due to her beauty.

"Okay..." she dragged as she slowly turned to walk away.

Promise wasn't too fond of Hassan, but since she was the head nurse and he was the head doctor, she would always be cordial because they had no choice but to work together.

"Sorry about that. I was deep in thought." He caught her before she could walk away. "How are you today, Promise?"

"Well, as always." She smiled, showcasing her pearly whites that a barely noticeable clear retainer covered.

"Good to hear."

There was nothing left for either of them to say, but Hassan knew he wasn't ready for Promise to walk away just yet. Clearing his throat, he stood to his full height of six feet four inches, towering effortlessly over Promise.

"I never had a chance to apologize, for how things transpired during our first encounter." He started, and Promise stood there quietly looking up at him.

"You made the right call, and I am thankful you went against me, so for that, I wanted to apologize for the way I handled things." He smiled, and when he did, a faint sound left Promise's lips. She wasn't sure what it was or why, but his smile was now making her feel some type of way.

"Thank you, Dr. Davis." Her voice came out quiet and muffled, nowhere near as vocal and confident as when she sat in his office. Something was happening with her.

"You can call me Hassan."

Why would I do that? Promise thought, but she didn't say what she was thinking. "Okay."

There was nothing else left to say, yet Promise couldn't move her feet, though her brain was telling them to move. She and Hassan just stared awkwardly at each other.

"Dr. Davis?" they both heard his name being called, which briefly drew them from the trance they were in.

"Yeah?" he questioned, taking a final look at Promise before looking past her in the direction his name was called.

"You're needed in room twelve," they both heard.

"Hope to see you before the night is over." Hassan smiled before brushing past Promise. His words alone caused butterflies in her stomach.

What in the entire fuck? she thought as she turned around and watched him walk away. Before he walked into the room, he turned and winked his eyes at her, causing her more confusion.

"Seems like Dr. Davis has the hots for the charge nurse," Promise heard an X-ray tech tease as he sat on the other side of the desk watching everything that had just unfolded.

"Shut up, and mind your business," she quickly responded before walking away.

Promise wasn't sure what was up with Hassan. She damn sure was confused as to why he had her feeling a certain type of way when she didn't even like his ass.

PROMISE STILL HAD five hours left of her twelve-hour shift, but she was extremely bored because the night had been so quiet, which, to a sense, she was happy about. Since she didn't have anything to do, she walked into the on-call room, hoping to increase her word count on the book she had been writing.

"Oh, sorry." She apologized when she flipped the light switch on.

Promise noticed Hassan sprawled out on the bottom bed of the single bunkbed that sat in the room. He slept with one arm resting on his stomach, and the other behind his head supporting it.

"Sorry." She apologized again as she prepared to back out of the room.

"Hey," he called out as he sat up. "You don't have go."

"Umm," she nervously mumbled.

"I won't bite you."

Promise couldn't help but laugh as she walked in, closing the door behind her before sitting on the small love seat. The on-call room was small and really not comfortable, but most people went there to sleep, so they didn't care how big it was.

"I really didn't mean to interrupt you. I just wanted to work on my book since it's pretty chill tonight," she revealed sweetly, holding up her notepad and pen.

"You didn't interrupt me. I wasn't really sleeping anyway, more so resting my eyes, since you can't really get comfortable on these thin ass mattresses." He gestured to the paper-thin twin mattress he lay on.

"True." Promise laughed in agreeance as she prepared to start writing.

The room fell eerily quiet, so Promise started writing. She couldn't focus because she could feel Hassan staring at her.

"What?" she questioned without looking up from her paper.

"Look at me," he said, but his tone was calm and inviting, so Promise reluctantly looked his way.

"You're beautiful." He complimented, admiring her beauty. This was different.

So are you, Promise thought.

"Thank you." She couldn't help but blush, though she was trying her best not to.

Hassan just sat admiring Promise. He admired her roasted-toffee skin paired with hypnotizing, round eyes that looked animated, her natural, high cheekbones that appeared to be contoured, and her set of kissable lips that covered her impeccable set of teeth. She was effortlessly beautiful.

"How old are you?"

Why? Once again, he had Promise confused.

"Twenty-five."

The room once again fell quiet.

"How old are you?" She found herself asking, needing to know.

"Thirty-one," he quickly answered as if he was waiting for her to ask him. "May I ask you a kind of personal question?"

"Sure…" Promise dragged with a raised brow.

"You have a man?"

Just as the question rolled off his tongue, Hassan's pager went off. Simultaneously, there was a knock on the on-call room door.

"You both are needed back in the ER. We have head-on collision victims en route, and all the trauma rooms are open with all hands on deck needed," one of the doctors said, looking at Hassan but addressing them both.

Hassan and Promise both jumped to their feet, heading out the room. Never saying a word to the other, they were back in work mode. Hassan hoped he'd get the answer to his question later and could only hope she was single.

PROMISE AND HASSAN were walking out of the hospital side by side. The air was cool, birds were chirping, singing their morning song, and the sun was just rising for the start of another day, though theirs was ending.

They had worked together all night and pretty damn well. They had managed to save every person that came into the ER involved in the head-on collision. They both were ecstatic about the outcome, but they knew they wouldn't always have such great luck, no matter how hard they tried.

"You and I make a great team." Hassan beamed as he slowed his stride before completely stopping. Promise followed suit.

"Yeah, we do," she agreed.

"Even if we only work well together when I am following your commands." She smirked.

"C'mon now, I apologized about that."

"You did, you did." She nodded her head as she smiled.

"What?" she asked, confused as her smile slowly faded. He just stared at her.

"You never answered my question earlier since we were interrupted."

Promise knew what question he was talking about, but she scrunched her face, tilted her head, and looked to the sky as if she was trying to remember the question. Hassan chuckled. He knew she was pretending she didn't know. He watched her and already could tell she was one to never forget a thing; hence the reason she was a phenomenal nurse.

"Do you have a man? Married? Boyfriend? Attached? Girlfriend?" When he said that, he watched Promise's eyebrow raise a little, seeming insulted.

"Any of those things, or even something I didn't mention?" he continued with a smile.

Promise was twenty-five, and she had a few flings, even a one-night stand, but as far as a real boyfriend, someone she could see herself spending the rest of her life with, she'd never met someone like that. Tyriq was the closest thing to that, and that was years ago.

"I'm single," was her simple response.

"We're just going to have to change that, aren't we?" He winked, continuing to smile.

"Nope. Really don't have time for a boyfriend." She quickly dismissed. "But I have got to get going."

She started walking away.

"Same place tonight?" She tossed over her shoulder, referring to them having to work again tonight.

Without waiting for an answer, she strolled to her car without even looking back.

Hassan was one who would get something when he wanted it. He was just that determined. He wanted Promise. Promise may have shot his shot down this time before he had a chance to even make his move, but he wouldn't give up.

She would be his.

Chapter
Twenty-One

July 24th, 2011
Three days later...

It was Friday around three in the afternoon, and it was finally Promise's day off. Promise just knew that after she dismissed Hassan, he would pursue her the next day, but to her surprise, besides work, he hadn't said much to her.

She didn't know how to feel about that. The first day Hassan ignored her, it bothered her a little, but now, she was back to not giving a damn. His feelings and emotions were too wacky for Promise.

Promise was on her treadmill, running at a speed of 3.5 mph as she did five days a week when her cell phone began ringing. She didn't know the number, so she ignored it. Just as quickly as she ignored it, it rang again. This time, she answered, but she never slowed her stride on the machine.

"Hello?" she answered breathlessly, placing the phone on speaker.

"Did I catch you at a bad time?" she heard a deep, commanding voice ask, and she knew it was Hassan.

"Ho-How did you get my number?" she stuttered, slowing her stride on the machine before coming to a complete stop.

"I got it from the employee roster at work. I hope that wasn't a problem."

"Yeah, it is…" She started but quickly stopped.

"I mean, I just wish you would have asked me for it, rather than looking on the roster." She corrected truthfully.

Hassan knew he was already taking a chance by calling her. He had dialed her number multiple times, hanging up before it rang. He finally said fuck it, and actually let it ring until she answered.

"You're right," was his simple response.

"So… what can I help you with?" she asked as she walked to her refrigerator, grabbing her Fiji water.

"Are you busy tomorrow?"

"No," she dragged, thinking maybe he was calling to ask her cover a shift, but she found that a weird since he, too, was off and because most times when they wanted her to cover a shift, the head nurse on the shift would be the one to call.

Hassan cleared his throat before he spoke, "Well, I was calling wondering if I could take you out tomorrow night?"

"Like a date?"

"Yeah, like a date." Hassan chuckled.

Promise had already told him she wasn't looking for a relationship, so she didn't understand why he would want to take her on a date.

"I don't see why not." She sighed.

Promise didn't realize how horrible her reply sounded until it was already out, and now it was too late.

"I mean, I don't want you to feel obligated to do a thing

you really don't want to," he said, not missing her tone and little interest.

"No… I do want to," she said a little more enthused than she wanted to.

"Okay. Pick you up at six," he said more as a statement than question.

"Sure."

"Okay. I will call tomorrow for the address."

"Okay," Promise replied before they said their goodbyes.

"Oh my gosh!" she squealed as she leaned against her kitchen counter.

It was true she wasn't interested in a relationship. In fact, she wasn't interested in even giving a guy the time of her day right now, but it was something about Hassan that had her wanting to get to know him on a more personal level.

Twenty-Two

July 26th, 2011

Promise stood in her bedroom looking at herself in her cheval mirror. She had changed her clothes so many times and still really didn't like what she had on, but she would have to wear it since Hassan would be there any minute.

Promise was wearing a red, long-sleeved bodycon dress that stopped mid-thigh with six-inch, nude faux-suede platform heels. Promise was rarely in anything other than scrubs since she worked so much, but when she did get dressed, she killed the game.

Just as she was tossing her bone-straight hair over her shoulder, her phone began ringing. She knew it was her best friend Nicole because of the ring tone.

"Hey," she answered, placing it on speakerphone while sitting on her king-sized bed, crossing her legs.

"Are you already on your date?" Her husky voice blared through the speaker.

"No." Promise laughed.

"He should be here soon though," she added.

"Well, good. You have your location turned on your phone?" she asked.

Whenever they went on a date, they both always tracked the other's location. Nicole didn't need her location tracked lately since she had been a relationship for almost two years with a guy named Carlos. She and Mario split not long after high school.

"Of course," she said while laughing. "Hey, he's calling. I'll text if I need you to get me away."

"Okay. Have fun, be safe, and I love you."

"I love you too," she responded before quickly hanging up, answering her other line.

"Hello?" she answered.

"Okay, I am coming down," was her response when Hassan said he was pulling up.

Hassan may have wanted to come in, and she probably should have invited him—hell, normally, she would have—but for some reason, she didn't.

"WHAT DID YOU THINK?" Hassan asked as he and Promise sat close together, snapping their fingers in approval of the poet that just finished his piece. They were at an open mic night at a lounge in Virginia Beach.

"Deep." She sighed in amazement.

"Tough topic, but it was amazing," she added with a smile as she picked up her apple martini, taking a sip.

"Yeah, it is a tough topic, but sadly, that's the reality for us black men."

"True." She nodded her head to the music that began playing.

"What?" she nervously asked when Hassan drank his Amaretto sour. He would normally have something stronger, but since he was driving, he was going easy.

"Nothing."

"Then why are you staring?" She hated being watched.

"Just trying to figure you out."

Promise smiled politely.

"Instead of trying to figure me out, how about you just ask me what you want to know?" She crossed her legs and placed her drink back down, before crossing her arms as if to say she was waiting for him to ask whatever he wanted to know.

"Ah… feisty." He chuckled. "Are you attracted to me?"

"What?"

Promise heard him loud and clear, but she was confused. She just knew he was going to ask her something about her, like maybe her favorite color or food. She wasn't expecting the question he was asked.

Hassan didn't repeat himself. He just leaned back in his chair, placed his leg over his knee, and grabbed his shoe, adjusting his leg, just looking at her.

"Umm, yeah," she finally whispered, tucking her hair behind her ear.

She had never really given thought on whether she was attracted to him or not, but looking at his smooth, brown skin, neat shoulder-length locs, tattooed arms, and perfectly structured face had her seeing what she never paid much attention to. He was actually fine as hell.

"Why?" she found herself asking.

"I just want to make sure I am not wasting my time," he quickly responded.

"You aren't," she lowly mumbled.

They both fell quiet, and after what seemed like an eternity but was only a few seconds, Promise spoke again.

"Am I wasting my time?" She pursed her full lips together waiting for an answer.

"Nah, that's not something I do," he replied without batting an eye.

"Okay" Promise bashfully smiled as she bit her bottom lip.

"As long as we're on the same page." He winked his eye at Promise, and her smile only widened.

They were finally on the same page.

Chapter
Twenty-Three

August 2nd, 2011

"Has anyone ever told you, you have the most beautiful eyes?" a male patient named Charles asked Promise as she stood over him, taking his vital signs in the ER.

"Thank you." She blushed as she looked over at Hassan after he cleared his throat.

She and Hassan had been hanging out and conversing since their date. They were getting close.

"Whoa!" Charles exhaled deeply when the blood pressure machine read that his blood pressure was 205 over 105.

"You're so fine. Being in your presence got my pressure all high and stuff." He joked, laughing a thunderous laugh.

"Are you having headaches or blurred vision?" Promise ignored his statement.

"I was having blurred vision with a horrible migraine. Well, that was until you walked in here." He winked.

Promise smiled a friendly smile. She was used to getting

compliments, hit on, and even asked out on dates while working, sometimes even by women, but with Hassan in the room, it felt awkward.

"Nurse Montgomery, thank you," Hassan spoke as he grew tired of his patient hitting on Promise. "Mr. Charles, how long have you been having these headaches?"

"I don't even know," Charles mumbled, looking at Promise's butt as she washed her hands.

"Mr. Charles!" Hassan was a lot louder than he normally was, but when he followed Charles's eyes and saw him eye-fucking Promise, it made him furious.

"Could we focus for one minute? Please." His voice a lot calmer than before.

"Whatever you say, boss." Charles put his hand to his forehead, saluting Hassan.

"What did you ask again?" he questioned, and though he said "whatever you say boss", he still wasn't paying attention.

Charles half listened as Hassan asked questions and explained what labs and tests they would run.

"Is pretty lady going to do all of my tests?" he asked, looking over at Promise, who now stood close to the door, holding his chart.

"Her name is Nurse Montgomery." Hassan quickly corrected him. "But yes, she will be the one helping you with all of the things I have ordered to be done."

"Well, that's all that matters." He smiled.

Hassan shook his head in disbelief before looking at Promise.

"Could you draw some labs, collect a urine specimen, get him hooked to an ECG, and lastly, go ahead and start an IV of saline so we can get the dehydration under control," Hassan rambled off, looking at the chart he had taken from Promise while occasionally looking up at her to make sure she understood what he was instructing.

"Sure." She barely nodded before watching Hassan walk out the room.

"Pretty lady, he your boyfriend?" Charles asked, nodding toward the door Hassan just walked out of.

Promise laughed nervously. She started gathering all the materials she would need to start some of the things Hassan had ordered.

"No," she replied.

"Does he know that?" Charles chuckled.

Promise didn't respond, but she could see why Charles asked. The way Hassan had just acted showed differently.

THE REMAINDER of the night Hassan was distant with Promise, and she didn't understand why.

"Did I do something?" Promise asked as she stood near Hassan, waiting at the ambulance entrance for an ambulance that had been dispatched to them.

"Why'd you ask that?" He looked over at her just after he tightened the string on the sterile suit before wrapping his big hands in the sterile, purple gloves.

"You just seem off since that one patient a few hours ago."

Hassan chuckled. "Nah, you didn't do anything."

Promise was about to respond, but the loud sounds of sirens indicating the ambulance was near halted her words.

"Keep ya game face on." He looked over and winked at her.

"Wow," Promised mumbled, side-eyeing him.

How was it he was barely talking to her, just brushed her off, but now, he was winking his eye at her? She just didn't get it.

Chapter
Twenty-Four

August 5ᵗʰ, 2011

Promise started distancing herself from Hassan since that one day. She wasn't sure what was up with him, but she knew she didn't have the time for it. She was an adult and wouldn't act like anything less than that.

With a bowl of frozen yogurt, she sat down Indian style in the middle of her bed. Today was her day off, and she had plans to chill in her bed all day watching Netflix.

After scrolling, she finally settled on what she always watched—*Grey's Anatomy*. It was something about that show that, no matter how many times she watched it, she couldn't get over it.

Ding!

Just as she scooped her favorite treat onto the spoon, her phone chimed. Placing the spoon into her mouth upside down and leaving it there, she unlocked her phone. It was Hassan.

Hassan: *Hey. Everything good?*

Promise: *Yup.*

Hassan: *Umm... you sure? You been MIA lately. Not only that, you're kind of short with me right now.*

Promise laughed at his message.

"I just don't have time for the wishy-washy stuff," she spoke, taking the spoon from her mouth.

He seriously must have forgotten how he acted the other day for no reason and then tried to pretend like everything was okay.

Promise: *Yup.*

Promise watched as the three dots appeared in a bubble, indicating Hassan was typing. It quickly went away but appeared again before it went away and didn't come back.

"Whatever," she muttered, not really having time for it.

Just as she tossed her phone to the side, it dinged again. Hassan had messaged her again.

Hassan: *IDK what's going on, but I am headed to you*

"Ummm, what the hell?" She chuckled because he didn't even ask, he just told her. She was just about to respond when there was a knock at her door.

"Oh, wow."

She climbed out of bed, heading to answer her door. Promise hated that her hair was in a loose bun on top of her head. She wore a tank top covering her braless breasts, boy shorts that barely covered her ass, and her feet were bare. Of course she was at her own home, but with Hassan at her door and them never having sex, she hated how he was about to see her, but he was the one who popped up uninvited.

Exhaling, she unlocked her door before opening it.

"Hey." She stepped back, and he stepped in.

"I ain't mean to just come back without asking permission, but I had to come clear the air." He turned, facing her.

Promise didn't know what to say, so she just stood near her door, looking up at him. They weren't in a relationship, so why did he get mad the other night? Why was he even here now explaining himself?

"I wanted to apologize because of how I acted the other night when we had that patient." He started, and Promise smiled a little because she wasn't for sure at first, but with him saying it, he confirmed he was jealous the other night.

"I know we aren't in a relationship, but hearing and watching him gawk over you fucked me up a little," he admitted, and Promise could see it was a bit hard for him to even say.

Promise still didn't know what to say, so she stood quietly.

"I was immature, and I just hope you forgive me."

The room fell silent, so Promise knew it was her turn to talk.

"I just want to know that our friendship won't be ruined with us working closely together because some patient or even coworker hits on me. I know we aren't in a relationship, but we're kicking it, so I would never disrespect you. I can't tell other people what to say out of their mouths or how to act, but as I said, just know I would never disrespect you."

"Okay." He nodded.

"So we good?" she whispered, looking up at him, her long natural lashes batting.

"We're good." He smiled.

Promise didn't like that he had just popped up, but after talking, she was grateful that he did.

Chapter
Twenty-Five

August 18ᵗʰ, 2011

Hassan kissed Promise, savoring every moment. Everything about her was amazing. They were at Hassan's condo. Her skin was soft. Her hair smelled like freshly whipped shea butter. Her breath always smelled of mints. Her smile lit up the room. Promise was beautiful; she was magical.

Today was Promise's birthday, and had it not been for the flowers that her parents had sent to her, nobody would have even known.

"You want to do this?" Hassan broke the kiss, peering down at Promise.

He only asked because he felt her small hands reach under his shirt. Hassan was more than ready, but he needed to make sure this was what she wanted.

"Yes." She slowly nodded her head as she spoke.

Whether she was ready or not didn't matter, because

right now, her center was dripping and begging to be touched.

Hassan smiled and pushed a piece of hair from her face while stroking the side of her face, running his thumb over her full lips just before pressing his own against them. As Hassan slipped his tongue into Promise's awaiting mouth, he scooped her up in his strong arms. She wrapped her legs around his waist, and they never broke the kiss. The kiss never slowed or broke as Hassan walked through his house toward his room with Promise wrapped around him. Thankfully, he knew his house.

"You okay?" he asked in a concerned tone once they reached his room and he laid her in the middle of his bed.

Promise didn't say anything. Instead, she nodded her head. Hassan pushed her legs open with his knees as he pushed her form-fitting, thigh-length dress over her hips.

"Don't do that." Hassan pushed Promise's hands from her face when she covered them as he removed her laced panties. Though she'd had sex before, Promise was shy.

"Sorry," Promise mumbled, now embarrassed at her shyness.

"Don't be." Hassan licked his lips as he leaned down, kissing Promise.

Promise was only embarrassed because she hadn't had sex in forever, and she wasn't even sure if she could do sex anymore. She just knew she wanted it.

Hassan sat up for a moment, looking down at Promise as he bit his bottom lip, before taking two of his fingers into his mouth.

"Ahhh," Promise moaned and winched in pain at the same time as Hassan slowly inserted his fingers inside of her wetness. It was clear to Hassan that she hadn't sex in a long time, if ever at all.

"Damn," he mumbled after taking his fingers from her tightness, placing them in his mouth.

"Happy birthday." His voice was low and raspy as he positioned himself between her legs, his breath tickling the outside of her honeypot.

Promise couldn't say a word. They'd gotten caught in the back of her throat when she felt Hassan's tongue lick from the opening of her kitty to her swollen clit. *Oh my fucking gosh,* Promise thought just as Hassan cupped her ass with both his hands while sucking and licking her clit.

"Sss," she moaned, arching her back while grabbing at his locs.

Promise felt she didn't know how to have sex, but she knew for a fact she wouldn't know what to do with Hassan after the head she was getting. She wouldn't tell him that, but before tonight, she had never had her center pleased orally.

As much as she wanted to make the head last, Hassan was just that good. She was on the verge of cumming.

"Ha-Hassan, I'm," she stuttered unable to form a sentence.

"Oh my gosh!" She bit her bottom lip as her eyes rolled in the back of her head, and her flesh swelled between his lips.

Hassan quickly flipped her over on her stomach, barely stopping in between. He pulled her ass closer to his face before he inserted his fingers into her wetness as he ate her ass.

"Fuck!" she squealed.

"I'm cumming…" Her voice was muffled because she was facedown in the silk sheets that were half off the bed.

Not only was Promise cumming, but she was doing something she hadn't ever done, even when she masturbated —squirted. Hassan never slowed his movements. He kept them steady, which caused her to cum and squirt hard. It was a good thing he couldn't see her face, because she was everything but pretty.

"Damn, boy." Promise collapsed on her stomach when Hassan stood from the bed.

Promise knew she should have turned around or made some sort of effort to let him know she was ready for him to enter her, but from the way she just came, she couldn't do shit but lay there as her hair stuck to her face.

Hassan smirked as he undressed before reaching into his nightstand and grabbing a condom. He quickly tore it open before sliding it down on his manhood that stood at attention with the veins pulsating. He was ready to feel her.

Positioning himself behind her, he grabbed the sides of her waist, pulling her back to him before slowly entering her. Promise was tight. Thankfully, she was wet. Otherwise, Hassan probably wouldn't have been able to enter her.

Just as Hassan got his rhythm going, Promise already felt herself about to cum since he was hitting her G-spot.

"Fuck," Hassan heard her muffled voice.

Grabbing ahold of her hair, Hassan wrapped it around his fist while grabbing one side of her hips as he thrust his. The sound of slapping skin and Promise's moans filled the room.

Promise didn't even bother announcing it as her warm juices from her cumming coated the condom that was wrapped over Hassan's dick. Hassan could have held out, but Promise felt like a slice of heaven, and he was having his piece. He was enjoying it. He sped up just a little, and moments later, grunted as he came hard.

After a few seconds of basking in the moment, Hassan removed his manhood from her still-pulsating center just before removing the condom and getting off the bed and going into his bathroom. Once again, Promise collapsed where she was. This time, she didn't even have the little energy from before to move.

Hassan had just put it down, with both his tongue and

dick. He had just confirmed it was more to sex than what she had experienced in the past.

Flipping her over once he was back in the room, Hassan gently cleansed Promise with the warm washcloth he had just brought back from the bathroom. That was also a first.

After cleaning Promise up, Hassan climbed his naked body into bed beside her, pulling her to him, and she rested her head on his tattooed chest before quickly falling asleep.

"Happy birthday, beautiful," he mumbled, kissing the top of her forehead before he soon fell asleep too.

Twenty-Six

August 19ᵗʰ, 2011

Birds chirped, and the sun shined bright through Hassan's bare floor-to-ceiling windows, which caused Promise to slowly open her eyes. Adjusting her eyes to the light in the room, Promise shifted her weight, slowly easing out of Hassan's arms, careful not to wake him. She climbed her naked body off the bed, going into the bathroom.

Sitting down to pee, Promise couldn't help but to smile as last night's events played in her mind. She was already digging Hassan before last night, but hell, after that, she low key was in love. She wouldn't tell him that.

Damn, he fucked the shit out of me, Promise thought as she stood to wash her hands. No other dude she had sex with was a match to Hassan, no matter what.

"Good morning," Hassan said as soon as Promise emerged from the bathroom while he sat with his back against his plush headboard.

"Good morning. Sorry. I didn't mean to wake you." She sincerely apologized.

As Promise walked back to the side of the bed where she had slept, she felt Hassan watching her. When she looked over, sure enough, his eyes were glued to her.

"What?" Her self-consciousness she tried to hide on a daily was on front street.

"You're so damn beautiful," he spoke, causing Promise to blush just as she climbed on the bed beside him.

"Thank you."

"You don't have to say thank you, because trust, this entire relationship I am going to say it often, and I'm sure you will get tired of saying thank you." He chuckled.

Promise giggled at his words as she pulled the thick comforter over her body.

"Relationship?"

Are we in a relationship? she thought, just looking at him waiting for an answer.

"Hell yeah," he stated.

"After the way shit went down last night, it's a must. I put my name on it and claimed what's mine." He laughed but was serious.

Promise's giggles turned into full-blown, stomach-hurting laughter. Funny thing was, Hassan said it, but she thought it.

"Okay," she whispered as her laughs subsided.

"But first thing's first as we kick this relationship off."

"What?" she nervously asked.

Hassan leaned over closer to her. Promise was positive he was going to kiss her, so positive that she puckered her lips, but the kiss never came.

"That shy shit from last night, that's got to go."

Promise had heard that she needed to be more confident a lot through her life, whether it be her work or just herself in general. No matter how hard she tried, her shyness outshined the little bit of confidence she housed.

"Okay," she mumbled, her shyness coming off as embarrassment showed.

"Promise, you're beautiful. You have to let it show just as much as others see it." He reached up, stroking her cheek, this time leaning in for a kiss that she didn't see coming.

"Okay," she once again mumbled when the pair finally broke their passionate yet short kiss.

Promise would try. Hell, she had never stopped trying. She could only hope one day she felt as pretty as everyone always said she was and had the confidence she knew she lacked.

Chapter
Twenty-Seven

August 26th, 2011

Tonight was a slow night. It was bittersweet. They didn't have anyone coming in, so it meant there was no one to possibly lose, but it was horrible because that meant the dragging twelve-hour shift felt more like a thirty-six-hour shift.

"I know you have all the ladies, Dr. Davis," a lab technician said.

The ER staff was sitting around the desk just chatting about being in relationships with the single ones saying how many people they dealt with at a time.

No one in the hospital knew Promise and Hassan were dealing with each other, and they both preferred it that way. It was less drama they had to deal with.

"Nah, I don't," was his simple reply. He answered the lab tech but was looking at Promise.

"You have a girlfriend, Dr. Davis?" a nurse chimed in, looking at him while batting her fake lashes.

Promise knew the nurse only asked because she was hoping for a shot at him. They all threw themselves at him.

"Yeah." He nodded his head with his reply while winking his eye at Promise.

"Seriously?" Disappointment was evident in her voice. Her face surely proved it if her voice didn't.

Promise couldn't help but blush as she tucked her top lip under her bottom lip, trying her best to hide her smile.

"What about you?" Promise heard, but it didn't register that the X-ray tech that had been trying to get with her for a few months now was talking to her until he nudged her.

"Me?" She faked a cough, her face turning red as all eyes were fixated on her.

"I mean, you're sitting over there all quiet," the nurse who asked Hassan did he have a girlfriend quipped.

"Yeah. Do you?" Hassan sat up on the edge of his seat. He enjoyed messing with Promise.

"Since y'all must know," she rolled her eyes harder than she needed, "yes, I am in a relationship." She blushed. She hated that all eyes were on her.

"Is it serious?" Hassan asked. The smirk he wore on his lips also showed in his eyes.

Promise felt everyone's presence. Hell, she knew they were there, but staring into Hassan's deep-set, dark eyes, all she saw was him.

"I'd like to think so," she mumbled.

"I just hope I'm not fooling myself," she added, nervously biting her lip.

"It's serious, and you aren't fooling yourself." Hassan confirmed, now standing. Promise couldn't help but smile.

"Dr. Davis!" they heard, causing them to snap out of the trance they were in from gazing deeply into each other's eyes.

Without a word, they both looked in the direction that Hassan's name was called.

"What are you doing? We have ambulances en route from a multiple-car accident," the other ER doctor said, looking at the pair as if they were from another species since everyone else was frantically running around while they were just staring at each other.

"Let's go," he quickly said, immediately going into work mode.

Neither knew what their relationship would become, but right now, it was clear they were on cloud nine with no signs of coming down.

Chapter
Twenty-Eight

Promise lay sideways on the bed with her head resting inside of her palm. She watched Hassan sit on the side of the bed after discarding the used condom since they had just finished having sex.

The lion tattoo on his back looked as if it roared whenever he moved. Hassan's full sleeve of tattoos covering his right arm from his shoulder down to his wrist along with his shoulder-length locs didn't give a first impression of a doctor. He was a sure case of not judging a book by its cover.

Not only was he a trauma doctor at just thirty-one, he had graduated from Mayo Clinic School of Medicine, which only accepted fifty students at a time. He graduated at the top of his class. He even spoke both Spanish and German fluently.

He was fine and educated.

"What are you smiling at?" Hassan asked as he looked back at her before sliding back onto the bed.

"You just make me happy," she admitted.

Hassan was the vocal one in their relationship, so hearing Promise say something so simple yet meaningful caused him to smile.

Hassan lay on his back, pulling Promise on top of him before brushing hair from her face that had fallen forward during the move.

"You're so special to me." He kissed her lips. "I want to introduce you to my parents."

Promise gasped at what he said. She knew if Hassan wanted her to meet his parents, she had to really mean something to him.

"You think we're ready for that?"

"Why not? You planned on dipping on me?"

"No." She giggled.

"Me meeting your parents must mean this is serious?" She pointed between the two of them. What she said came off as more of a question than a statement.

"You don't think we are?" he asked, though he had told her multiple times they were serious.

Truth be told, Promise never gave it much thought. Of course, Hassan made her happy, gave her phenomenal sex, and treated her the best she ever had been, but besides knowing he was her boyfriend, she never gave their relationship much more thought than that.

"What do you want out of this relationship?" Hassan questioned before Promise could answer his first question.

Promise bit her bottom lip while shrugging her shoulders.

Hassan sat up a bit, looking down at Promise. He knew what he wanted to say, but he was thinking so he could choose his words wisely.

"Baby." He started, clearing his throat.

"Baby, I know what I do and don't want in life. Right now,

I want you. We aren't getting married next week, but know that I ain't in the business of dating just for fun. I am searching for my wife, the mother of my children, someone I can grow old with, my forever." He paused, letting his words sink in.

Promise gasped before swallowing hard.

"You want to marry me?" she asked in a childlike voice, surprised by what she had just heard. They hadn't even exchanged I love yous yet.

"Eventually." Hassan's voice was confident, and his eyes spoke just as loudly as his mouth did.

"Right now though, I want you to meet my parents," he quickly added when he felt her body slightly tense under his touch.

"Okay." She smiled.

"So when?" she asked, lifting her head to look into his eyes.

"They're having their huge annual Labor Day barbeque, and I was hoping since you were off, you would go with me then." Hassan knew Promise was off because they worked the same shift and schedule.

Promise didn't think she was ready to meet them. He was trying to introduce them when there were lots of other people around, causing her hesitation to grow.

"Okay." She smiled, not wanting to make a big deal about it.

Chapter
Twenty-Nine

September 5th, 2011

"Baby, relax." Hassan reached over, touching Promise's bare biscotti-colored thigh as he pulled in front of his parent's huge house.

"I am relaxed." She lied while smoothing over her red matte lipstick.

Promise knew this day was coming almost two weeks ago, but now that it had finally arrived, she was nothing less than a ball of nerves.

After placing the car in park and stepping out, Hassan casually walked around to Promise's side. He opened the door for her, taking her hands into his before walking around the back of his parents' home.

Old-school music filled the backyard. As some people danced to the beat, some stuffed their faces with the assortment of delicious foods while others drank the many alcohols that filled a table. The vibe was fun yet mellow.

There was one particular couple that caught Promise's eyes. They danced to the beat that played, but they looked different than the other dancers. They looked so in love.

"Those are my parents right there." Hassan pointed out the couple that stood out to Promise.

After a good look, Promise could see the man looked like an older version of Hassan, just without the locs. The woman was petite with a silver-gray colored bob. When she smiled, a lone gold tooth sparkled. She was beautiful and stylish.

"Hassan!" she shrieked when she twirled and noticed her son.

"OG!" Hassan leaned down, hugging his mother strongly with one arm, never letting go of Promise's hand.

Hassan has always called his mother OG. He used it so long he wasn't sure where it came from or how it started.

"Pops!"

His father pulled him into a strong, manly hug. Again, he never let go of Promise's hand.

The hugs were finally out of the way, and both of Hassan's parents stepped back, eyeing Promise, neither uttering a word. Promise hated being the center of attention, but it felt like all eyes were on her.

"And who is this stunning young lady?" His mother was the first to speak. She never took her eyes off of Promise.

Promise couldn't help but smile and blush. Hearing someone as beautiful as Hassan's mother compliment her beauty made her feel good.

"Promise."

"This is my girlfriend." Hassan introduced.

Promise held her hand out politely to shake Hassan's mother's hand, but to her surprise, she bypassed her hand and pulled her into a hug, releasing her soon after.

"Sweetheart, we have heard so much about you."

Promise looked up at Hassan, and he smiled down at her. He had been talking about her.

"He told us you were beautiful, but I must say, beautiful is an understatement."

Promise blushed even harder. Her cheeks began to burn from how wide her smile was.

"You can call me Sharon." She finally said her name.

"And you can call me Herbert," Hassan's father spoke for the first time as he, too, pulled Promise into a hug.

"It's nice to meet you both." Promise enjoyed the fact that both Hassan's parents liked her, but it was also weird how they had already taking a liking to her as if they had known her a while.

"Hassan, get y'all some food and drinks, and dance," Sharon said, looking to Hassan before turning her attention back to Promise.

"Let him take care of you. You come sit with me."

Promise heard so much behind *let him take care of you*, but as usual, she smiled and nodded right before being tugged away by Sharon, leaving Hassan and his father in the middle of the yard.

"I can't believe your room is like you never left." Promise laughed as she sat Indian style in the middle of Hassan's queen-sized bed, looking around his room that still had the *Word Up!* and basketball posters on the wall.

"At what age did you move out?" She teased, picking up a stuffed bear that was in the corner on the bed and tossing it, which he caught.

"You got jokes." He tossed the stuff animal back, laughing.

"I'm happy your parents liked me. At least I got the feeling they did." She quickly changed gears.

Not many people disliked Promise. She honestly didn't care either way, but it mattered to her if Hassan's parents liked her or not.

"Baby, you're dope." Hassan walked toward her.

"I told you they would like you," he added, stroking her cheek as he grabbed her foot, pulling her to the edge of the bed to where her legs dangled off the side, and he stood in between them.

"Now that's out the way, we should stop hiding our relationship." Hassan only kept their relationship a secret out of respect for Promise, but now, he was ready for everyone to know she was off the market and belonged to him.

"Can you meet my parents first." What she said was a question, but it came off more as a statement.

"No doubt, baby."

"What?" Promise nervously laughed when Hassan only looked down at her while stroking her cheek.

"Whachu tryna do?" He licked his lips before running his hands through her long tresses as he massaged her scalp lightly.

"In your parents' house?" she whispered, shocked he would even want to have sex there, especially while they were home.

"They damn sure know we ain't virgins." He teased before leaning down to kiss her.

"Plus, their bedroom downstairs. They ain't worried about us in the least bit," he spoke when the kiss broke.

"Hassan," she moaned when she felt his tongue snake from her neck up to her ear, his breath tickling her the whole time. He was definitely hitting her spot.

Promise wanted to be strong because she felt it was weird to have sex in his parents' house, but after one touch too many, a kiss that lingered, and a body that was begging to be touched, she found herself being undressed. She even helped with undressing Hassan so they both could take each other to ecstasy right in his room that hadn't been changed since he was in high school.

Thirty

September 19th, 2011

"Who in your family do you look like?" Hassan asked as they lay in the hammock in Hassan's backyard.

The pair had just gotten back from Hassan meeting Promise's parents. It was clear that Promise didn't look like either of her parents and not just because she was adopted. Her parents were dark, where she was light. Her mom was heavyset; Promise was small. It was so much about them that was different that it stood out they weren't her real parents or at least one of them wasn't.

Promise had been dating Hassan for a while, and she had plans to one day tell him about her being adopted, but she didn't tell that story often. Though she wasn't biologically related to her parents, they were nothing less of that.

"I don't know," she whispered with a shrug.

"What do you mean?" Hassan was confused.

"Promise not to look at me different?"

"Never."

Promise was nervous, but Hassan was her boyfriend. She felt he deserved the truth.

"My parents adopted me when I was ten years old. They aren't my real parents."

Hassan saw the look on Promise's face. He knew she was embarrassed.

"Do you know your real parents?"

"No," she quickly answered, her voice coming off as a high-pitched scream.

"They gave me away, so I never had a desire to know who they were since they obviously had no desire to be my parents," she added a lot calmer and slower.

Hassan didn't say a word. He saw her lips moving, but no sound came out, so he sat quietly, allowing her to get it together.

"When I was younger, I always asked the normal questions; why did they give me up? Why wasn't I good enough? Or would they ever come back to get me? But as I got older, I realized I didn't need an answer to any of those questions, because my parents that God sent me had everything I thought I wanted from my birth parents."

Her voice cracked. It was obvious that though she wore it well, the pain she felt was still fresh and heavy.

"You're already looking at me different." She nervously laughed.

"Baby, I'm not." Hassan sat up before standing, pulling her to her feet, looking down at her while towering over by more than a full foot and a half. "I'm not looking at you differently. You're just amazing. Baby, you don't look like what you have been through."

Hassan was right. Promise didn't look like any of what she experienced in her short twenty-six years she had been on earth.

"Yeah… Well, that, along with numerous other things, I have pushed to the back of my mind and have learned to pretend it didn't happen."

"I get it, baby." He kissed the top of her forehead.

"No pressure, but if you ever want to talk about that or anything else you pushed away, I am always here to listen," he said in a reassuring tone.

"Okay." She smiled up at Hassan, her doe shaped eyes glistened with the tears she had fought. Hassan pretended like he didn't see them.

"You're amazing." Hassan kissed her soft lips, causing her to purr just a bit under his touch.

He couldn't change her past, but he was sure going to aim to perfect her future.

Chapter
Thirty-One

October 15th, 2011

Promise's hands sweated, her mouth was dry, the hairs on the back of her neck stood up, and her heart was racing, but she held her head high, trying to hide her emotions. She walked beside Hassan into the ER's consult room where a family was patiently waiting for an update on their family member.

A twenty-two-year-old male had come into the ER after a head-on collision with a tree. He wasn't wearing a seat belt and was highly intoxicated since it was his birthday. Hassan, another doctor, and Promise, along with her nursing staff, did everything they could to save him, but his injuries were too significant, and he succumbed to them.

"Ready?" Hassan questioned, looking over at Promise.

How the hell can anyone ever be ready for something like this? she thought, looking up at him.

"Whether I am or not, we have to do this," she mumbled.

Normally, only the doctors would be giving the sad news,

but Hassan volunteered Promise since the two of them were the first ones in the room when he was brought in by the ambulance.

"Remember, show no emotion." He reminded her as he knocked on the door and stepped in.

Holy fuck.

It was so many people in one room. When they heard the door open, they all stood with hopeful eyes. Sadly, Promise knew those hopeful eyes would soon turn into hurtful, tear-filled ones.

"My name is Dr. Davis, and this is my head nurse, Nurse Montgomery." Hassan introduced as he slightly turned to Promise when he introduced her.

"How is Phillip?" a family member, who Promise assumed to be his mother, asked anxiously.

Hassan cleared his throat.

"We did everything we could to try and save Phillip, but his injuries were too severe, and he sadly passed at 0300 hours." He said, referring to military time as they always did.

It seemed like the air in the room had been sucked out for a second as family members began to cry. Moments after Hassan dropped the bomb, Promise heard the most gut-wrenching scream, one she would never forget, come from the lady that asked how Phillip was.

"Not my baby!" she cried just as she lost the feeling in her legs. Thankfully, someone was there to catch her before she fell.

"I'm sorry for your loss," Promise heard Hassan say to the family, and she knew she should have said it too, but she didn't want to speak and risk letting the tears she was holding in fall.

"The chaplain will be in to speak with you all, and then you will be able to see Phillip if you would like."

"Yes, yes, of course," someone spoke.

"Again, I am sorry for your loss."

"Sorry," Promise managed to mumble before quickly turning out the room.

"Promise, wait up," Hassan said, damn near running after Promise, but she didn't stop.

"Promise," he called out, following her into the on-call room.

"I-I can't. I can't." She hyperventilated while grabbing at her chest.

"Breathe, Promise. Deep breaths," he coached.

"Deep breaths in and out," he added, demonstrating what he was telling her to do while pulling out a chair for her so she could sit down.

Tears fell fast down Promise's light-colored skin, but her breathing was slowly returning to normal as she peered into Hassan's eyes, inhaling and exhaling deeply.

"You okay?" he asked, reaching up and wiping her tears with his thumb as he squatted in front of her.

"Death has never scared me. Ever. I can deal with a lot, but not being able to save that man on his birthday, hearing you break the news to his family, and then hearing his mother's scream. Now that... that's what scared me." She sniffled.

"It's never easy."

"Clearly." She threw her hands up because of how much of a mess she was after delivering the news. She was over it.

"I love being a doctor, especially in a trauma department, but if I'm honest, which I am, that is what I hate most about my job. It was your first time having to do something like that, and you may not feel like it since you're crying now, but you handled yourself well," he said with a smile.

"Not only did you handle yourself properly, we did everything we could to try and save him, so don't feel like you didn't." He reassured her.

"Oh my gosh." She exhaled deeply.

Hassan didn't want her stressing over something neither of them could change, so he leaned in to kiss her. Just as he was slipping his tongue into her awaiting mouth, the on-call room door flew open, causing them to break the kiss and turn in that direction.

"Dr. Davis?" a nurse squealed. She seemed shocked and disappointed.

Though Promise and Hassan had agreed to tell everyone about their relationship, they chose not to do so at work because he didn't want anyone saying he gave her special treatment because they were in a relationship.

"So sorry," she mumbled, backing out the room, letting the door close a little harder than needed behind her.

"Welp, you know after Tell-It-All Tina just saw us kissing, the entire ER will know now," Promise said in a joking tone.

Tina couldn't hold water, no matter the secret or who it belonged to.

"Yeah, well." Hassan shrugged. "Let's get back to work."

He leaned down, once again kissing her, before turning on his heels with her in tow. There was still work to be done, even after the breakdown.

Chapter
Thirty-Two

October 27th, 2011

"What is this about?" Hassan was the first to speak as he and Promise sat in the head of the ER department and chief executive Chuck Fontaine's office.

Mr. Fontaine was an older, black man with salt and pepper hair, a small frame, and big voice. He didn't look like he should be in charge of anything.

Mr. Fontaine cleared his throat. Before then, he had never had to speak with Hassan or Promise. In fact, this was his first time seeing Promise.

"First off, I want to tell you both, thank you for all that you do and have done in the ER. The job you guys have to perform on a daily isn't one for the faint or weak. I appreciate you."

"But?" Hassan questioned. He wasn't stupid. He knew they weren't sitting where they were sitting together to just be told thank you.

Promise sat quietly, not saying a word. In situations like this, she tended to observe more than anything.

"It has been brought to my attention by a few of your colleagues that the two of you have a relationship leaning more towards a personal rather than professional one." He paused for a second, but neither Promise nor Hassan spoke or budged.

"You two are adults and free to do what you like outside of this hospital, but you both know fraternization has never and will never be tolerated here," he added. "You signed an agreement on that when you were hired."

"Are you firing us?" Hassan questioned.

"Of course not, Dr. Davis," Mr. Fontaine quickly spoke. He knew he couldn't afford to lose either of them.

"So what then?" Promise finally spoke, which caused Hassan and Mr. Fontaine to look her way.

"Because you two have a relationship outside of work and since it was also said that you show Ms. Montgomery special treatment over the others, I have one of three things that will need to happen."

"We're listening." Hassan sat up in his chair.

"One of you can switch to day shift or to another department."

"What's the third? You said one of three things," Promise once again spoke.

"One of you can transfer hospitals. But with you all's great work ethic, I would hate for either of you to switch to another department or another hospital for that matter."

"What if we told you the complaints are lies and we have nothing going on?" Hassan questioned. At this point, neither of them had admitted nor denied their relationship.

"That would warrant an investigation to determine the allegations to be true or not. But let me say this, Dr. Davis and Nurse Montgomery, it will be extremely hard to determine otherwise, when multiple staff have made a complaint. The two of you have been seen leaving together multiple times, always working closely together, and once seen outside of work together."

"That's proof we're in a relationship?" Hassan chuckled.

"It is not. But the fact that neither one of you denied the allegations here and now tells me otherwise. Not only that, the two of you were caught kissing in the on-call room by one of your colleagues."

Both Promise and Hassan looked to each other, knowing it was Tell-It-All Tina who blabbed about the two of them. They knew she couldn't hold water on telling other peoples' business. They just didn't know she was a snitch too.

The room fell quiet with Mr. Fontaine assuming the pair were trying to make a decision and Hassan and Promise not really thinking anything.

"What would you two like to do?" he finally asked after realizing they weren't going to say anything as they stared back at him.

Promise looked to Hassan, and he reached over, grabbing her hand. There was no need in pretending they weren't an item when it was already out.

"What do you want to do?" He stroked her hand.

Promise smiled. She liked how he was giving her the option to lead.

"Do you want to stay on nights?" she asked him. She knew leaving the ER or hospital for that matter wasn't an option for either one of them since they loved the trauma department and the hospital itself.

"Whatever you want to do, baby." He lifted her hand to his lips, kissing it softly.

Promise smiled.

"Days it is." She looked to Mr. Fontaine with a shrug.

"Okay..." Mr. Fontaine dragged as he wrote something down.

"Nurse Montgomery, your new shift will start immediately."

"Okay," she mumbled.

"I truly hate having to do this." He apologized.

"Are we done here?" Hassan questioned, not even acknowledging his apology.

Hassan wasn't upset per se. He just hated they were being reprimanded for their relationship.

Mr. Fontaine peered at the pair over his glasses. They were done, but he was just observing the two of them.

"I just wish you both well."

"Yeah, thank you." Hassan stood, and Promise followed suit.

"Welp." Promise shrugged once they were outside of Mr. Fontaine's office. "This is why I was hesitant about telling anyone about us."

"Baby, it's cool. I mean, shit, yeah, we will no longer be on the same shift, but that won't affect our relationship at all." Hassan reassured Promise.

Promise nervously laughed. "Good thing today was our day off. That way I can hopefully get adjusted to day shift."

"Baby, I could have taken the days." He pulled her to him.

Promise smiled up at him and relaxed when he wrapped his strong arms around her body.

"I know, baby, but it's cool. One of us had to do it."

She reached up twirling one of his locs around her finger.

"It's going to be hard not seeing you as much anymore."

"Agreed." Hassan sighed.

"But we gonna make some shit shake," he added just before kissing her.

They would see each other less, but Hassan had plans to change that as much as he could, and soon.

Chapter
Thirty-Three

November 1st, 2011

"Time of death 2032." Hassan's voice was full of sorrow as he stepped back from the small, lifeless body.

"Shit!" he cursed, snatching off his face mask.

A two-year-old boy had been vacationing with his family at the campgrounds in Williamsburg when he walked to the edge of the lake, falling in while they barbequed outside of their RV. It was almost seven minutes before the family realized he was missing.

"You did everything you could," a new nurse said with tears in her eyes as she tried to be comforting to Hassan.

"Thank you," he mumbled, barely paying her any attention.

She was sweet, but he knew since she was new, she had a lot to learn.

"Tina, let's go." He turned his back to head out of the

room. She would be with him when he told the family since she was the first one to touch the little boy when he arrived.

Without a word, Tina dropped her head and followed Hassan with her feet shuffling the entire way.

Loud cries filled the tiny room as Hassan delivered the devasting news. Hassan wasn't a crier, but the sound of pain from losing a loved one at such a young age tugged hard at a place in his heart. Hours ago, they had been enjoying each other on a family vacation. Now, they would be carrying their son home in a casket.

"Again, I would like to send my heartfelt condolences," he whispered, touching the shoulder of the boy's brokenhearted mother before reaching out shaking the stunned father's hand.

"Someone will be in shortly to take you to him," were his last words to the family before quickly turning on his heels to leave, the life sucked out of the room.

"Dr. Davis?" Hassan heard his name being called, and before hearing his name, he had forgotten Tina was with him when he spoke to the family.

"What?" He stopped but didn't turn around.

"I know you're upset, so tell me what I can do?" Tina sounded genuinely concerned.

"Tell me, please." She reached up, touching his strong tattooed arm.

Hassan wasn't dumb. He saw right through her fake concern and bullshit.

"What can you do?" He chuckled, but no smile touched his lips.

"You can stay far away from me. Had you not gotten the best thing on this night shift moved to days, that little boy would probably still be alive."

"What?" Tina was insulted and confused.

"Promise would have intubated to get an adequate flow of

oxygen the moment she touched the little boy. You did not. Promise would have never needed to trade off after only ten minutes of performing CPR, and you did, which caused us to lose time. And Promise damn sure wouldn't have been encouraging me to call time of death on a two-year-old little boy, who still had a full life ahead of him like you did." He roughly pointed at her.

"So what you can do for me is stay the hell away from me, be the LPN your ass went to school for, and leave the doctoring to me," he huffed with gritted teeth before turning to walk away.

Tina stood there, speechless. The tears that didn't come earlier were surely forming now, but she exhaled deeply before turning in the opposite direction to walk away. Hassan had touched a nerve.

PROMISE WALKED into Riverside Hospital almost two hours before her shift. Hassan had called her on his lunch break as he always did. Tonight, she heard the agony in his voice. She knew her man needed her.

As she walked in search of Hassan, she was stopped by a few night-shift staff, telling her the shift wasn't the same without her. She appreciated their kind words, but she also didn't give a damn about them. She had to find her man.

"Hey," she called out after pushing open the on-call room door, spotting Hassan laying on his back and looking up at the ceiling.

Hassan quickly stood when he saw her. Her hair was in a tight, high bun, her doe-shaped eyes appeared more slanted, and her cheekbones were higher than normal. She was only wearing her purple scrubs and black and purple Crocs. She was simple yet beautiful.

"What is it, baby?" she questioned when Hassan dropped to his knees, pulling her by the waist and crying on her stomach.

She had never seen or heard him cry. Whatever it was must've been hard for him.

"I tried everything. Everything I could," he stuttered.

"I tried so hard, but I couldn't save that poor little boy. I needed you here, baby, because I couldn't save him alone. He was only two. Two," he said between sniffles as she shook his head in disbelief.

Losing a patient was never easy, especially when it was a child, but he was taking this loss personal.

"I'm sure you did everything you could, baby." Promise soothed, grabbing his cheeks, lifting his face so his eyes could meet hers.

"You did everything." She wiped his tears as she, too, got on her knees.

Promise wasn't there to know he had given his all, but she knew how passionate he was about being a doctor and saving lives.

Hassan knew he did all he could do. It was just he and Promise were a better team, and if he had her tonight, things would have surely been different.

"What?" she asked when the tears dried and she could no longer read his facial expression.

Hassan tucked his lips before untucking them, slowly running his tongue across them both.

"Promise..." He started.

"Promise, I love you." He took her hands into his, intertwining their fingers.

When she heard those words, she gasped, and a smile crossed her perfect full lips.

"Not just love you, but I am in love with you," he added before Promise could say anything. She gasped again.

"I love you." She pressed both their hands towards his chest as she pointed her finger near his heart.

Promise did love Hassan, and it didn't just happen overnight. However, because she felt it may have been too soon, she kept it to herself, yet knowing he felt the same way warmed her heart.

The pain Hassan felt quickly faded. With a smile, he leaned in and kissed his girlfriend. She was just what he needed. With that kiss, the love they both confessed was felt all through it. They were made for each other.

Thirty-Four

November 16th, 2011

It was almost three in the morning when the ringing of Promise's phone awoke Hassan. It was both their off day, and they were at Promise's apartment.

"Baby?" He held her tightly in his massive, defined, tattoo-covered arms as she slept peacefully.

"Baby?" He tapped her when she didn't move the first time.

"Hmm?" she replied, her voice a little raspy.

"Your phone was ringing, but it stopped," he said just before the phone rang while vibrating on the nightstand again.

Quickly sitting up in the bed, Promise touched the lamp beside the bed, illuminating the room just enough to see before sliding the green button on her phone to answer.

"Daddy, what's wrong?" she nervously asked when she realized who was calling from the caller ID.

Promise heard her father ramble off a few things, but

what stuck out most was, "It's your mother. You need to get to Williamsburg Sentara now."

"On my way." She hung up the phone before hopping out of bed rushing to her dresser.

"I have to go." She had her back to Hassan as she took out a pair of black leggings, socks, panties, bra, and a gray thermal shirt, quickly slipping them all on.

By the time she turned around dressed, Hassan was sitting on the bed dressed in his gray sweatpants, T-shirt, and Nike Air Max.

"Baby, you don't have to go," she said as she brushed her hair into a ponytail.

"Yeah, I do." He watched her step into her Ugg boots.

"Ready?" He stood from the bed, walking toward her.

Without a word, she stood on her tiptoes, kissing him.

"Thank you," she said before they walked out the room.

She knew she didn't have to thank Hassan, but she knew she had to say it because she was thankful.

THE AUTOMATIC SLIDING doors opened as Promise and Hassan stepped in holding hands. When she spotted her father, she dropped Hassan's hand, rushing to him and hugging him tightly.

"Daddy, what's going on?" she asked, removing the fuzzy beanie she was wearing on her head.

"I got up to go to the bathroom around one-ish, and when I climbed back into bed, I noticed your mother didn't stir like she normally did when I would get out or back into bed. I tapped and called her name repeatedly, but nothing. I checked for a pulse. It was there, but very faint, so that's when I called the paramedics." Promise heard the defeat in his voice.

"Where is she?" Her voice trembled, afraid to ask because of the answer she may get.

"They're running some tests. I haven't been able to go back there yet."

Promise was just about to say something when a doctor and nurse walked out. The time stood still, the people around them disappeared, and her breathing stopped. This scene was all too familiar for her. Normally, she and Hassan and the other doctors were the nurse and doctor going to families of the victims. This time, she was the victim.

"Tell me my mother is okay." Promise looked into the doctor's eyes, hers hopeful.

Hassan grabbed Promise's hand. He knew the news wouldn't be good, but he wanted her to know he was with her.

"Your mother suffered a massive heart attack and a stroke. As a result of that, she is—"

"In a coma." Promise finished the doctor's sentence. She knew because of both things happening, her brain lacked the needed oxygen to perform, so it resulted in her mother falling into a coma.

"Yes, ma'am." The doctor nodded slowly.

"Are you a doctor?" she asked Promise.

"No. I am a nurse," she mumbled.

"Oh."

"Can we see her?" Joseph asked.

"Yes, sir. We're getting your wife settled into ICU. Once she is settled and the nurses have exchanged information, someone will be down to get you all," she said.

"I wish you all the best," she added before she and her nurse walked away.

"I have to sit down." Promise began feeling lightheaded as she started to hyperventilate.

"Relax, Promise. Head down, and deep breaths in and out." Hassan instructed, kneeling in front of Promise.

"Baby, she will be okay." Hassan smiled once Promise's breathing was back to normal.

"She will be okay," he repeated.

Promise could only hope Hassan was right, and her mother would be okay. She couldn't and didn't want to imagine life without her.

Chapter
Thirty-Five

November 16th, 2011

The trio was led down the hallway of ICU. Each door they passed resounded with the beeps of ventilators, heart monitors, or blood pressure cuffs and echoed the halls. Promise's heart sped up just when they reached room 3401.

"If you all need me, I will be at the nurse's station," a young nurse who looked to be in her early twenties with big bifocal glasses said.

"Okay," Joseph said just as Promise pushed open the heavy door that lead to her mother's room.

Whoosh, beep, whoosh, beep, whoosh beep, was the sound of the ventilator breathing, and the heart monitor counting the rhythm of the heart. Tears slowly fell down Promise's light-colored face as she neared her mother.

A breathing tube was down her throat, IVs that administered medicine in her arm, a blood pressure cuff that occasionally took her pressure encircled her bicep, and the tube from the catheter that caught her urine was visible.

"Mommy," she whimpered once she was near her.

Promise knew her mother couldn't respond to her, but she also knew that while in a coma, a person could hear everything. Sometimes hearing their loved ones helped pull them through.

"It's me, Promise, Mommy." She put her lips close to her ear. "Mommy, I need you. Please don't leave me. Don't leave Daddy. Daddy needs you. Rest now, Mommy, but please come out of this. I need you so bad."

Promise stopped, briefly wiping her mother's cheek because her tears had fallen on them.

"I love you so much." She kissed her warm cheek.

A warm presence came over the room as Promise stood back from her mother. She couldn't explain the feeling, but something told her everything would be okay. Promise stepped back, allowing her father access to her mother. Once her father started talking to her mother, she grabbed Hassan's hand, leaning into his chest, realizing he was the love of her life. Just like she didn't want to lose her mother, she didn't want to lose him.

"I love you," Hassan said before she could as he kissed the top of her forehead.

"I love you." She smiled up at him, tears still in her eyes.

"She will be okay." Hassan confirmed what she was already feeling. She could only hope they were right.

Thirty-Six

November 22nd, 2011

It was two days before thanksgiving. It was supposed to be a happy time. For Promise and her father, it was everything but that. They felt they had nothing to be thankful for.

Not much had changed with Promise's mother except a few days ago she had taken a turn for the worst, where they weren't sure if she was going to make it.

"Mommy, they're wanting us to take you off the machines soon." Promise's voice cracked as she stood next to her mother's bed. She was there alone.

"You have to pull through. I might sound selfish, but I can't lose you. I know you may be tired, but Mommy, please fight a little while longer." She sniffled.

"Remember when I was thirteen and I broke my femur bone because of the tumor, and every day you prayed I would be okay and could dance again? Well, Mommy, the tumor was benign, and I pulled through and continued to dance for you. So Mommy, please do this for me," she begged.

The room fell silent when Promise stopped talking and dropped her head. Only the sound of all the machines could be heard.

"I remember when I first came to live with you guys…" Promise started again.

"I swore you hated me." She giggled. "I was like this lady is just like the rest of them places I have been. They pretend to nice at first and then turn into monsters. I gave you so much trouble the first couple of months, but your soft-spoken, sweet demeanor changed how mean I was to you. I want you around, Mommy, but I understand if you can't fight any longer. I will know it wasn't because you didn't try. Instead, it will be you fought all you could and just won in a different way."

Promise leaned down, kissing her mother's forehead while stroking her head.

"Be free, Mommy." She sniffled.

There was nothing she could do. Her mother had fought her fight, and it just may have been time for her throw in the towel, and as selfish as Promise wanted to be, she didn't want her mother holding on when she was tired of fighting.

As Promise walked out of the room, her mother's finger twitched, but Promise never saw that.

PROMISE COULDN'T SLEEP. There was a weird feeling in the pit of her stomach. She couldn't determine if it was a good or bad feeling. Her phone vibrated. When she looked at the time on the nightstand, she realized it was almost the exact time her father had called saying her mother was in the hospital.

Her heart skipped a beat when she picked up her phone and saw it was her father.

"Hello?" Her voice was shaky.

Tears rolled down Promise's face. She even screamed without knowing causing her to wake Hassan up.

"What is it?" he asked in concerned tone.

"She's woke," she said in disbelief as she looked back at Hassan.

"She is asking for me." She smiled with tears still falling.

"Then let's go." Hassan hopped out his bed.

"Okay. Okay." Promise was really in disbelief, but she got dressed because she had to see it for herself.

It was almost too good to be true for Promise as she looked on at her mom sitting up in the hospital bed as if she hadn't been in a coma for the last few weeks.

"Promise." Marilyn reached her hand out toward her.

"Yes, Mommy." Her voice sounded childlike rather than the adult she was. Marilyn grabbed her hand.

"For you, baby, I will always fight." She smiled at Promise as tears welled in the bottom of her eyelids. She had heard Promise.

"I love you." She finished.

"I love you so much more," Promise cried.

"Hassan?" She turned her attention from Promise to him.

"Yes, ma'am?" Hassan's voice was deep and filled the room as he stood next to Promise.

"The answer to your question is yes," she said smiling at him, and Promise looked between the two of them confusingly, but she didn't ask what they were talking about, because if she was to know, they would have told her.

Today was a good day. Promise, her father, and even

Hassan couldn't be more thankful that Marilyn was awake. That was one less thing that they had to worry about.

Chapter
Thirty-Seven

December 25th, 2011

Hassan: *Hey, baby! How is it going?*
        Promise: Hey, baby. It's going okay. Wish I wouldn't have agreed to pick up a few hours on Christmas. I'd rather be at home in bed with you. 😴 Promise sent back.

Hassan: LOL! Yeah, baby, me too. It's cool though. Only a few more hours.

Promise had picked up a quick, six-hour shift since they would be short, but it was technically her day off.

Promise: True. Are we leaving from your place or mine? She sent, referring to them going to her parents' for dinner.

Hassan's parents would be there as well. This was the first time both families would be together.

Hassan: You have everything you need here at my house?

Promise: We'd better leave from my mine, LOL!

Hassan: I figured, LOL! Once I am done here at the gym, I'll just head to your place.

Both Promise and Hassan had a key to each other's place and came and went as they pleased.

Promise: Alright, baby. I'll see you in a little bit.

Hassan: Okay, sexy! I love you.

Promise: I love you more with your fine ass. 😄 Promise sent with a wide smile on her face.

———

PROMISE HAD LESS than thirty minutes left before her shift was over, and she was more than ready to go. The morning had been slow and boring.

"Where is everyone?" Promise asked out loud as she looked around the emergency department.

All of the next shift staff was supposed to already be there so they could go over shift notes although there weren't many since only two patients came in, and they both were sent home.

Just as Promise was passing the nurses station, the door from the lobby flew open.

"Nurse Montgomery! We need your help out here!" Dr. Whipple, the day-shift ER doctor, shouted.

Promise ran in his direction. Her ponytail rocked from side to side with each step.

Stepping out into the lobby, Promise stopped dead in her tracks when she spotted Hassan standing in the lobby dressed in a suit, one hand his pants pocket, and a serious look on his face.

"Ha-Hassan?" she muttered, walking to him slowly.

It wasn't until she was near him that she realized that their parents were there along with the hospital staff.

"Hassan?" she repeated once she was near him.

"Promise," he mocked her as he kneeled to one knee.

"Baby, you came into my life like a fireball. You didn't back down from me, even when I told you to. I don't say this often, but I am forever grateful you followed your gut and not my call. You're strong willed and determined, and because of that, it makes you this amazing woman that you are."

Promise was now shaking as tears fell from her eyes quickly. She now understood what was going on.

"Baby, we're a team. Together, you and I make incredible things happen. You're the yin to my yang. Without you, I am nothing. So, my beautiful, feisty queen that does not take crap from anyone, I am asking you today would you do the honor of becoming my wife? Will you marry me?" He smiled up at Promise, pulling out a black, velvet box and opening it, exposing the 5.03 carat platinum, octagonal-baguette halo diamond engagement ring, which was impeccable.

Promise knew the question was coming, but even when he asked, she gasped. Wiping her tears, though more fell, Promise reached her small hands touching the sides of Hassan's clean-shaven face. She slowly nodded her head.

"Yes! Yes, baby. Of course." Her words finally caught up.

Hassan slipped the ring on her finger before standing to his feet, lifting her from hers in the process. He kissed her deeply and passionately, almost forgetting they were in public.

"I love you, baby." He smiled at her after breaking the kiss.

"I love you more." She smiled with tears still falling as he placed her firmly back on her feet.

Promise looked around the room at everyone clapping, and her eyes landed on her parents. They both were crying. Her mother placed her hands to her colored lips, kissing them before extending them to Promise. Promise smiled as she returned the gesture.

A proposal was the last thing she was expecting on this Christmas day, but she had to admit, it was the best, unexpected present she had received.

Thirty-Eight

December 27th, 2011

"Hey, Mommy." Promise greeted her mother after she kissed her cheek before sitting down in the fancy, white chair.

They were having lunch at *Le Yaca* French Restaurant—their favorite.

"How are you feeling?" Promise asked just as the waitress walked away from taking their drink orders.

"I'm fine, baby," Marilyn said, but Promise didn't stop staring.

"Promise, I am fine," she said a little more seriously as she reached out, grabbing her left hand.

"You mother is fine child." She smiled.

"Okay," Promise mumbled.

Promise hated being a worry wart, but the thought of almost losing her mother scared her, so she had to make sure at all costs she was okay.

"Still on cloud nine about the engagement?" Marilyn

asked, changing gears as she pointed to the massive engagement ring.

"I am, Mommy." Promise smiled widely, but it slowly faded.

"What's wrong?" Marilyn saw the scared yet nervous look in her daughter's eyes.

"Mommy, please don't take this the wrong way, and I won't do it if you tell me not to," Promise rambled. Now was the time to tell her about the plans.

"What is it?" she asked in a concerned tone.

Promise took a deep breath.

"Hassan and I will marry soon and eventually have children, and you're my mother, no questions asked, but I want to find the lady that birthed me." She paused, but when Marilyn didn't flinch or say a word, she continued.

"I have so many questions I need answers to. But Mommy, if you don't want me to do it, I won't. I don't want you mad at me," she added, not taking a breath.

Marilyn was bought some time on her response when the waitress came back to get the food orders.

"Sweetheart, you know me well enough to know I will never be mad at you. The choices you make in life may not always be the ones I think you should make, but your father and I raised you the best way we could, so I know you will make the best decision." She smiled at Promise.

"You wanting to reach out to your birth mother won't hurt me at all because I am your mother. Yes, she carried you, but I am the one that made you into the woman you are today." Marilyn was confident, and she had every right to be.

"Whatever you need help with, I am always here," she added.

"Mommy, are you sure?" Promise questioned.

She wanted to find her birth mother but not at the

expense of ruining one of the best things that ever happened to her.

"Remember that day when I had woken up from my coma, and I looked to Hassan telling him yes?" Marilyn ignored Promise's question.

"Yes." Promise scrunched her face from confusion.

"He had visited me once without you. He spoke about how much he loved you and wanted to give you the world. In that time of speaking highly of you, he said he knew how much you valued my word because everyone else could say yes, but if I said no, then you wouldn't do it. Well, baby, before he asked you to marry him, he whispered in my ear asking could you be his forever." Marilyn smiled widely.

"I say all of that, Promise, to say, yes. Find the woman who birthed you, get all the answers you need, and know that I am behind you."

"Okay," Promise whispered, not realizing she was crying until a tear dropped and hit her hand.

"Okay, Mommy," she added.

She was right, no matter what. If Promise didn't have her mother's blessing, she wouldn't do any of it.

"I love you, baby girl." Marilyn stroked her hand.

"I love you too." Promise sniffled.

Promise had her mother's blessing, so now it was time to search for the lady who felt like Promise wasn't good enough.

Chapter
Thirty-Nine

February 3rd, 2012

"Mhmm, baby," Promise moaned as Hassan slowed his motion as his manhood slowly went limp.

He had woken her up with amazing morning head that sent her over the top followed by death strokes to her center, causing her to run from him and try to climb the wall. He wasn't letting her get away though, no matter how hard she had tried.

"You sure know how to make a girl enjoy the start of her next four days off, Dr. Davis." She teased while biting her bottom lip as she watched him head to the bathroom to dispose of the condom.

"I aim to please." He winked his eye at her just before walking in.

After disposing of the condom and cleaning Promise as he always did, Hassan sprawled his naked body across the bed. His body was a pure work of art. It was strong and toned. His arms were thick and defined, and he had a strong back and perfect ass. Tattoos covered a lot of his body, but Promise's favorite two were the lion's head that covered majority of his strong back and the full sleeve that flowed from his right shoulder down to his wrist.

Promise rested her back on his plush headboard as he lifted his head and rested it in her naked lap before she began to play in his freshly retwisted locs. Hassan was drifting back to sleep when he heard a squeal from Promise.

"What's wrong?" he asked, facing her and looking up, seeing her eyes glued to the screen of her iPhone.

"I think I may have found her." She turned her phone to face Hassan so that he could read the message she had just read.

"You think it's really her?" Hassan now sat up in the bed beside Promise.

"I don't know." She shrugged. "It has to be though. She's the right age, right city, last name, everything."

Promise had thought she had found her birth mother once before, but after further digging, she found out it wasn't her. She had become hopeless.

"Only one way to find out, baby," Hassan said. "You just have to message her to see."

Hassan supported Promise. He wanted her to get that closure she needed. Not only that, but he knew they would never marry until she closed that chapter in her life, and he understood why she had to close it.

"Yeah," Promise mumbled.

She had heard Hassan, even knew she should have messaged the lady that popped up as the match for her birth mother, but for someone reason, she couldn't bring herself to do it.

"I'll message her," she said, more so trying to convince herself.

She would message her. At least she was hoping she would.

IT WAS ALMOST MIDNIGHT, and Hassan was sleeping peacefully as Promise sat up in the bed with her MacBook Pro open, deleting and restarting an email.

Ms. Jennifer,

My name is Promise. I am emailing you because I am in search of my birth mother. I am unsure if you're her, but your name was a hit within my search. If you're not her, I want to apologize in advance. But if you're my birth mother, I would like to talk to you further. Thank you for your time.

Sincerely,

Promise Montgomery, R.N., B.S.N

Promise read the email over and over again as she nervously bit her bottom lip. She thought about removing her credentials from her signature just for this email but decided against it. She thought if it was her birth mother, she needed to see how far she had gotten without her.

Before closing her eyes tightly, Promise slid the curser over to the send button and without a second thought, she clicked send. Unlike the other times, she felt this was the person. Even if it wasn't, the email was sent, and there was nothing she could do about it now.

Promise was just about to close her MacBook and snuggle close to her man when her MacBook chimed, indicting she had an email. Her palms began to sweat as she opened the email.

Promise,

You don't know how long I have searched for you. Each time I thought I found you, it would end with disappointment. I want to apologize for ever giving you up, but Promise, you have to under-

stand, I was young, and my head space wasn't right, so giving you up felt like the best thing to do. I am truly blessed that you, too, were looking for me. Promise, I am hoping we can someday meet. I'm sure it won't happen overnight, but I want a relationship with you. I am also sure your little brother and sister would love to meet you as well. I won't hold you long. Here is my number, (757)123-4567. Call or text me anytime.

Again, I would love to meet you.

Hot tears fell from Promise's eyes. She thought she needed some questions answered, but after reading the email, she was upset that she even was on a hunt to meet Jennifer.

She has other kids? Promise couldn't help but think. How was it Promise wasn't good enough to keep, but she went out here and had more kids after her?

Swallowing hard, Promise closed her MacBook before setting it on the nightstand and sliding down in bed. Without opening his eyes, Hassan wrapped his strong arms around her body, pulling her to him. Promise relaxed in his arms.

Though Promise had wiped the tears, they continued to fall until she fell into a deep sleep.

Forty

February 4th, 2012

"I found her," Promise mumbled as she slid her phone across the island, showing her mother the email. They stood in Promise's parents' kitchen.

"You don't seem happy." Marilyn observed after she read the email.

"Mommy, I just don't know." Promise sighed.

"I thought finding her would make me happy or at least relieved. that I could ask her all the questions I have always wanted to. But after reading the email and knowing that she has more kids and is continuing on with life without me, happy or relieved is far from what I feel," Promise admitted.

"I only wanted to find her because I don't want to go into a marriage or become a mother harboring this hate I have for her, but Mommy, I didn't realize how deep the hurt and hate was until last night," Promise continued, and Marilyn let her speak without saying a word.

"I can't meet her, because I don't like her."

When the room fell silent is when Marilyn decided to speak.

"Promise, it's okay to not like her, even hate her as you put it. You were ten years old when she left you at that police station. Sweetheart, that was only sixteen years ago. You have every right to feel how you feel. But remember, you're doing this because you're an amazing person, and you want to continue being that amazing person. Yes, the pain is still fresh, but baby, you're doing this for you, and your future." Marilyn's tone was soothing.

"So you're telling me to still meet her?"

"No, baby. I am telling you to do what you feel is right. I can't tell what to do. Your father can't. Your friends can't. Neither can Hassan. You have to make the choice you feel is best," Marilyn said, reaching over and wiping her daughter's tears.

Lately, Promise felt all she did was cry.

"As I said before, Promise, whatever choice you do decide to make, I back you 100 percent."

Marilyn walked around the island to her daughter, pulling her into a tight hug. She could tell that was what she needed.

Promise wept in her mother's arms. Everything she was feeling came out in that moment. After crying, she knew what she had to do, even if deep down she didn't want to. It was the right thing to do.

Chapter Forty-One

February 8th, 2012

"Baby, are you sure you don't want me to go with you?" Hassan asked Promise as he watched her quickly walk around his room trying to find something to wear.

It was the day she would come face-to-face with her birth mother, and she was wreck.

"No, baby," she said, slipping into a pair of Levi ankle-cut jeans. "My location is turned on. We're meeting in a public area."

"Well, if I message you, and you don't message back, I am coming out there," Hassan said with seriousness.

"Okay." Promise kissed Hassan just after pulling her sweater over her head.

"I love you."

"I love you more!" she shouted back just before walking out the room.

Promise sat outside on the cold, wooden bench as she waited patiently for the stranger to arrive. *Relax, Promise, you have waited forever this,* she thought as she rubbed her sweaty hands on her denim jeans.

She had already been waiting for almost thirty minutes, and though she was early, she was now becoming impatient because the person she was meeting was now late.

"I don't even know why I bothered," Promise whispered with sadness in her voice after checking her iPhone.

The time displayed 3:35 p.m.; the person was now thirty-five minutes late. A slight pain ran through her chest as she stood to her feet. Even after all these years, things were still the same.

"Promise?" she heard her name faintly just as she was walking away from the bench, and she slowly turned around.

"Promise Lewis?" she heard. She almost said no because she hadn't gone by Lewis since she was ten years old.

"Yes?" she answered, her voice was shaky, and tears began to form.

"I'm Promise," she said, staring at the lady as her body began to shiver involuntarily as if she was cold.

"Oh… my… gosh…" the lady spoke slowly as she walked toward Promise before hugging her tightly once she reached her.

Promise wanted so badly to hug her back, but she couldn't bring herself to do it. She even wanted the hug to feel warm and safe, but it was everything but warm and safe.

"I'm sorry," the woman spoke, releasing Promise from the hug before wiping her tears. "Would you like to sit?" the woman asked, gesturing to the bench that Promise had just got up from.

Hell no! Promise wanted to scream, but instead, she

nodded her head before walking toward the bench and sitting.

"You're just like I always imagined. You're beyond stunning." The woman complimented her.

Promise only stared at her with tears burning the rim of her eyelids. However, she refused to let them fall.

"I am so glad you found me. I had been trying to find you for years," the woman continued.

I can't do this, Promise thought.

"Why did you abandon me?" she blurted out, looking at the woman as if she was crazy.

"I didn't ask to be in this world," Promise continued.

"I was your child, yet you threw me away as if I was trash," she added as she became angry.

"Ten years old, and you threw me away like I didn't mean a thing to you." She raised her voice while standing from the bench, feeling as though coming to meet this woman was a big mistake.

"How could you?" Promise questioned as she turned her back to the woman, unable to hold the tears back but refused to let her see her cry.

"How could you do that to your own flesh and blood?" she questioned with her back still to the woman as she thought back to everything leading up to this moment.

"I'm sorry," she whimpered.

"Jennifer, how could you?" Promise turned around, facing her.

Jennifer only shrugged. She didn't have a real answer as to why she did what she did, except a man.

"I understand your frustration, and I don't blame you at all. I just hope that one day, Promise, you can accept my sincerest apology."

"That day just won't be today," Promise hissed before

turning on her heels, walking away without another word. She had to get out of Jennifer's presence, and now.

Jennifer wanted to run after Promise. She wanted to hold her baby. Only thing was, Promise wasn't a baby, and this wasn't a fantasy. Instead, she stood still, watching Promise walk further away from her. She had made a bad call fifteen years ago, and she knew she may pay for it for the remainder of her life.

Forty-Two

March 2nd, 2012

"Here is the prescription Dr. Whipple prescribed. You will take this twice daily every twelve hours." Promise instructed her patient as she handed her a written prescription.

"If for any reason you don't get better or your condition worsens, please come back in immediately. Otherwise, follow up with your regular doctor," she added.

"Okay," her patient mumbled, not in the mood to talk.

"If you could sign your discharge papers right here." She tilted the steel clipboard toward her patient.

"Is there anything else I can do for you?" she asked with a smile.

"No, ma'am."

"Okay then. You have a wonderful day, and I hope you get to feeling better." She smiled before walking out the room.

Just as Promise walked out of the patient's room, her cell phone vibrated in her pocket.

Jennifer: Promise, please talk to me. Give me a chance to explain. Jennifer had been messaging her nonstop lately.

Promise exhaled deeply, quickly deleting the message. When she was about to shove it back in her pocket, it vibrated again.

Jennifer: Please? Just five minutes?

Promise: Fine. Meet me @ Newport News Park tomorrow at ten. You will have exactly five minutes.

Promise knew if she didn't reply, Jennifer wouldn't stop messaging her, even if she blocked her as she had before. Jennifer just messaged her from a different.

Jennifer: Okay. See you then.

Promise read the message while rolling her eyes before placing the phone back in her pocket. Jennifer would say what she needed to say, and Promise would send her on her way, so she could leave her alone forever.

Chapter
Forty-Three

March 3ʳᵈ, 2012

Promise sat in her car watching Jennifer as she took a seat at one of the picnic tables. Jennifer looked around, and Promise was sure she was looking for her. It had crossed Promise's mind to start her car and drive away, but something in her wouldn't let her do that.

Before getting out the car, Promise took a good look at Jennifer. She was beautiful. She looked a little older than she actually was, but otherwise, she was stunning.

Hassan asked Promise who did she look like, and now, looking at Jennifer, she realized she looked like her.

Finally, Promise climbed out of her car, closing the door. After hitting the lock button, causing the horn to beep, she walked toward Jennifer with her hands dug deep in her North Face fleece.

"I thought you weren't coming," Jennifer said once Promise was near.

"I started not to," she replied truthfully.

"Well, I am glad you decided to."

"What is it? Your five minutes has already begun." Promise's voice was cold as ice and almost froze midair before it reached Jennifer's ears.

"I had just turned sixteen years old when I had gotten pregnant with you. I was young. But your father and I knew what we were up against. Well that was until he was killed in a car accident three months before you were born. You wer—"

"You kept me for ten years though." Promise rolled her eyes, cutting her off, not buying into the story she was telling.

"I did. Promise, I am not perfect never pretended to be. Your grandmother, my mother, helped a lot. She helped us stay afloat, but when she passed away, a piece of me went with her. I still knew I couldn't do it alone, but I tried to be the best mother I could be at such a young age."

"What changed?" Promise asked.

Promise didn't remember much of her childhood. She tried to forget as much as possible due to all the pain it caused. She became numb to it.

"Slick, drugs, not being mature, or having my own mind. All of that. Your grandmother pushed me to do better, but when I lost her, my will to do better went with her."

"Slick is?" Promise vaguely remembered that name. She just couldn't remember how or why.

"He was my boyfriend. That was up until five years ago when he was killed for getting caught with someone else's wife."

Promise chuckled as she shook her head. "So a man allowed you to abandon your only child?"

"I was young, Promise. I am not saying it was right, but I was only twenty-six years old. I was—"

"The same age I am right now!" Promise hissed.

"I am not pregnant, but if I was, no matter my circumstances, I couldn't give up my child, and if I had to, I would have at least walked her inside the police station, rather than running away like a coward ass bitch," Promise said through tears as a vision of her being scared and alone outside of the police station watching her mother run away without a second look flashed.

"I'm sorry," Jennifer cried. There was nothing more she could say.

"Crazy thing was, even after you abandoned me, I hoped and prayed you would come back and get me. I would have forgiven you. I wanted you so bad that I wouldn't let my real mother love me." She spoke of Marilyn.

"I just want to say thank you for leaving me because had you not, I wouldn't have found the two most beautiful people who love me like their blood runs through mine." Promise now had tears of her own as she stared into Jennifer's eyes.

"I have hated you all these years, but looking at how pathetic you look right now, I don't hate you at all." Promise shook her head.

"I don't hate you at all," she repeated. Promise smiled. "I wish you nothing but the best in life. Also, I am unsure of how old your other children are, but I pray that you do a better job loving them than you did with me."

Promise stood there with tears falling as she watched Jennifer stare back at her crying her own tears. The five minutes Promise had allotted Jennifer had long gone, but with her getting out what she needed to, she didn't care about the time. But she had now said all she needed to, so she turned and walked away, leaving Jennifer standing there with her own tears.

Chapter
Forty-Four

March 10ᵗʰ, 2012

"God sure took his time and added too much sauce when he created you." Hassan licked his lips before sexily smiling at Promise.

Today was Hassan's thirty-second birthday, and he was having a small gathering at his house. He was seductively looking at Promise as she stood near his bar wearing a black thigh-length, spandex dress that peaked at her rose thigh tattoo. Five-inch gold heels were on her freshly manicured, size-six feet. Her hair flowed freely down her back. Besides the red lip stain on her full lips, she was makeup free.

"Thank you, baby." Her cheeks turned a rosy red from blushing.

It didn't matter how many times Hassan complimented her, he always caused butterflies in the pit of her stomach and made her feel good.

"Come here. Let me get you right really quick," she sexily whispered as she licked her lips.

Hassan wanted nothing more than to let Promise do her thing like she always did, but he knew once they got started, neither would just want to stop at oral pleasure, so with the little bit of strength he had, and boy was it small, he declined.

"Nah, baby. We both know we won't be stopping once we get started."

"Well, why don't we..." Promise started as she walked toward him before standing in front of him, unzipping his zipper to his slacks and slipping her small hand through the opening.

"Just tell them we are canceling." She ran her hand up and down the shaft of his large manhood that she needed two hands in order to cover its circumference.

Promise pulled his rock-hard manhood that had thick veins all over it through the opening of his slacks. Just after licking her lips, she dropped, squatting and opening her mouth, pulling Hassan into it.

"Sss, damn," Hassan groaned, reaching up to pull all of Promise's hair to one side as he watched her devour his manhood.

Ding dong!

"Fuck!" he cursed when the doorbell chimed.

"It's okay, baby. Your present will be waiting once everyone is gone."

She stood, wiping the corners of her mouth. She winked at him before sashaying to the door as he tucked himself back into his pants, watching her the entire way.

Yeah, he would kick their guests out early.

"So Hassan tells me the two of you have picked a date," Sharon said as she and Promise stood in the kitchen cleaning up a bit after the guests.

"We have," Promise smiled.

"It's set for December 25th this year."

It was only right that Christmas Day be the day that Promise take on Hassan's last name since that would make exactly a year since he asked her to be his wife.

"Such a beautiful thing." Sharon smiled, but Promise saw something in her eyes.

"What's wrong, Mrs. Davis?"

"What have I told you about that?" Sharon had once before instructed Promise to call her Sharon, but because of the way Promise was raised, she felt it was disrespectful to do so.

"I apologize," Promise said, and Sharon waved her off. "Something wrong?"

Promise was concerned because though she saw the smile, something in her eyes said different.

"Please forgive me in advance, and I hope I am not prying, but I have to say something."

"Okay…" Promise dragged, unsure of where Sharon was going with the conversation.

"You're a beautiful person, and I don't just mean your outer appearance. You spirit is beautiful and kind. Not only are you beautiful, but it has to be something special about you because Hassan have never brought a girl home. I'm sure he had some out there, but to him, they were never worthy enough to meet us. Baby, he brought you home because you're special and, as I said, beautiful."

Promise was confused as to where Sharon was going with her words, and it must have shown on her face because of Sharon's next words.

"I say all of that to say, Jennifer messed up in life, but you will have to let God deal with her. For the sake of your beautifulness, forgive her."

"I have forgiven her."

"Sweetheart, you haven't," Sharon quickly quipped. "If you had, you would be building some type of relationship with her. She is not your mother, you and I know that, but without her, you wouldn't be in the world and have the two amazing parents you have. She made a mistake, a horrible one, but let God deal with her. For your peace and sanity, forgive her. I am in no way telling you to forget, but genuinely forgive her."

"Yes, ma'am," Promise politely said, holding her gaze just as Hassan walked in.

"Hey, baby," she said smiling up at him.

"I've been looking for you. OG, I gotta steal her away so she can dance with me." Hassan grabbed Promise's hand leading her out the kitchen.

"Please think about what I said." Sharon winked at Promise just as they were passing her.

Promise smiled. She would think long and hard about what she had heard.

CHAPTER 45

May 12th, 2012

ear Jennifer,
I know I told you on our last meeting that I no longer hated you and I forgave you. The truth is, I lied.

Of course, I hate you. You deprived me of a real childhood with my mother. I remember crying myself to sleep, wondering why I wasn't good enough for you. I used to play in the mirror as a child pretending you had come back for me saying you didn't mean to leave me. When I was growing up, I needed you so much. There wasn't a day that went by that I didn't blame myself for you leaving.

Jennifer, I will never understand what you did, no matter what you or anyone else says, but I can't change what you did. Clearly, something or someone was more important than me, and that's okay.

For years, I have housed a hardened heart. Even when I tried to pretend I was okay, I wasn't. All I ever wanted was the love from my mother. I don't know my story. The memories I have from my childhood don't start until about eleven, and that's not okay.

You told me I have a little brother and sister. I can only pray that you do them better than you did me. I am almost positive that you aren't a horrible person. You just made some horrible choices in life. I refuse to carry the weight of wondering why for the remainder of my life.

Jennifer, this time I mean it. I do forgive you. I also hope that you can forgive me for the way that I have treated you. No matter my hurt and pain, it was not right. Also, though I forgive you, know that I will never forget.

It may take some time, but maybe one day, I can meet your other children. I may be almost twenty-seven, but I have always dreamed of being a big sister. You cannot replace the mother that has raised me into the woman I am today, but if you would like, I do want you in my life. You will never be called mom or anything like that, but I do want a chance for us to get to know each other.

Before I end this, I want to say thank you. Thank you for giving me life.

Sincerely,

Promise Montgomery.

Jennifer read the letter over and over again. Promise wanted a relationship with her. Though Jennifer couldn't change the past, she had plans to make the future a much better one.

Forty-Six

August 18th, 2012

"Happy birthday, baby." Hassan walked up behind Promise, wrapping his arms around her waist with two glasses of Moet champagne in his hands, handing one to her.

"Thank you." She turned around with a smile pushing her body into his.

"I told you I didn't need a party." She continued smiling, referring to the surprise party Hassan had thrown her at Legacy Hall.

"I know, baby, but I just had to. You have been so busy with work and planning our wedding. I felt like this was the least I could do." He kissed her forehead, and she melted under his touch.

"I love you," was all Promise could muster up.

"I love you more," Hassan repeated the words Promise always said to him. "Don't trip, but Jennifer just walked in."

Promise didn't even budge when she heard that Jennifer

had walked in. She was actually happy Hassan had invited her.

Turning around, Promise spotted Jennifer and two children, who looked to be around eight and eleven, stood near her. The girl looked older but identical to Jennifer while the boy had Jennifer's features but was darker in color.

Swallowing hard, Promise quickly downed the drink Hassan had given her before handing him the ice-filled glass and walking toward Jennifer and the two children.

"Happy birthday!" Jennifer shouted over the music once Promise was near before she handed her a wrapped gift.

"Thank you," she replied before looking between the two children.

"I am Promise. Your big sister." She introduced herself, smiling at Jennifer before hugging both children, who hugged Promise back while giggling.

"Thank you for coming," Promise mumbled sincerely just as she hugged Jennifer.

At first, the hug was light, but before either of them knew it, the hug became tight and warm. They had a long way to go, but they were on the right path for mending what had been broken a long time ago.

Chapter
Forty-Seven

December 25th, 2012

"Relax, bestie. You're marrying your king, whom you deserve." Nicole nudged Promise, noticing the nervous look on her face.

"Baby girl, ready?" Joseph asked, holding his hand out for Promise to grab.

"With you by my side, I am always ready." She smiled, taking his hand.

"Then let's get you married."

***

"All My Life" by K-Ci and JoJo played as Promise watched from her parents' back window as her wedding party walked down the long, snowy path in her parents' backyard.

Just before "Love Never Fails" by Brandon Heath started playing, Promise adjusted the white fur shawl on her arms.

"It's time, baby girl." Her father lifted her hands to his lips kissing them gently.

Promise simply smiled up at him just before taking her first steps down to her soon-to-be husband.

Brandon Heath belted "Love Never Fails" just as Promise reached Hassan, who wore a million-dollar smile. Hassan wore an all-white, three-piece suite with an iris flower tucked tightly in the breast pocket.

"We're gathered here today…"

The pastor started her speech, and Promise zoned out as she looked into the crowd of guests, spotting Jennifer and her brother and sister. She smiled at the trio. It took a lot of counseling, tears, screams, and dedication to build a relationship with Jennifer, but they were slowly coming together. Promise knew she would never call her mom or anything of that nature, but she was actually glad to have her in her life. She loved her little brother and sister.

"Promise, your vows," Promise heard the pastor say.

Before Promise could begin, she felt the tears burning the bottom of her eyelids as she looked in Hassan's eyes with a smile. She loved him dearly.

"'Promise, call it,' were your very first words to me, baby. I didn't even know you, and I truly disliked you, but baby, how times have changed." Promise's smiled widened. "Being with you, Hassan, shows me who I am. Even if I ever wanted to give up, I couldn't, because with you in my corner, quitting is not an option. You push me to be a better person. I love you because even when I didn't see my potential, you did. I wasn't looking for anyone, but God surely knew I needed you."

Hassan reached his hand up and over to Promise's face with a smile, brushing the tear from her face with his thumb.

"Hassan, your vows." The pastor's voice was shaky from holding back tears.

"Baby, you're strong. I don't mean physically; I mean mentally. You have experienced so much in life, but looking at who you are today and what you have accomplished, it doesn't show. You say I push you to be better? Well, baby, nah, I am better because of you. No matter what was thrown your way, good or bad, you have bossed up and handled it all. I couldn't be happier that I get to spend the rest of my life with you. God knew I needed you, baby.

"Promise, I am making a promise to you today, as long as I am alive, that no harm or pain will come your way if I have anything to do with it."

Chapter
Forty-Eight

December 31ˢᵗ, 2012

Promise sat on the sand with her toes sank in deep. The water crashed against her skin as she and Hassan were on their honeymoon in Bali.

It was just before eight. Promise had snuck out from under Hassan's arms. She didn't want to wake him as she went and just enjoyed the scenery. Sitting there alone, looking out at the pure blue water, she couldn't help but to cry happy tears. She had a man, whom she loved dearly, and he loved her equally—maybe even more—a great job, and a family that wasn't perfect, but it was all love.

"You trying to dip out on me already?" Promise heard Hassan's deep voice behind her, startling her from daydreaming.

"We haven't even been married a full week yet." He joked once Promise looked his way, shielding her eyes from the sun that was rising high.

Promise drooled at the sight of Hassan. Her eyes slowly roamed his body. His locs fell over his shoulders, and he was shirtless, exposing his hairless, chiseled chest. Her eyes fell lower to his rippled eight-pack that she loved running her small hands across. Biting her lip, her eyes fell a tad lower to his basketball shorts that sat low on his waist, exposing just a bit of his pubic hair.

"Mhmm." She looked at him hungrily when she saw his thick manhood through his shorts.

He wasn't even hard, but he was blessed. Lastly, her eyes fell to his calf muscles. Hassan was a doctor, but he had a body more of an athlete, a runner to be precise.

"Whachu tryna do, Mrs. Davis?" Hassan flirted as he squatted beside Promise, reaching his hand up, stroking the side of her face.

"You." She drooled.

He was her husband, and she wasn't afraid to tell him what she wanted.

Promise loved the fact that they were on a private island because they could make love wherever, whenever, and however; and they damn sure did. Promise had been beyond horny since before they left Virginia, and Hassan made sure to satisfy every inch of her body.

"Baby, are you okay?" Hassan asked, seeing Promise gag as if she was going to throw up twice.

"I just had a weird taste in my mouth. But I am fine." She backed away from Hassan with a smile.

This was the second time Promise had gotten sick since being on their honeymoon. Hassan was convinced she was homesick.

"You sure?" Hassan wanted to be balls deep in Promise, but of course, he wanted her not feeling sick and possibly actually throw up while she was riding him reverse cowgirl or anything.

Without a word, Promise leaned into Hassan, licking her lips seductively as she traced each one of his rippled abs before slowly moving her hand down inside his shorts.

"I said I'm good," she finally spoke once the weird feeling was gone.

Promise had turned Hassan on even more. Yeah, he wanted her well, but he also wanted her. She wanted him just the same. He was about to take her on a ride of her life.

"Baby, you haven't drank anything since we have been here." Hassan noted, placing his mixed concoction to his full lips.

"I know, baby," was her simply reply.

Hassan knew Promise wasn't a drinker, and neither was he, but most times, they did drink together. Lately, she hadn't.

"I am so ready for the fireworks." She changed the subject as she leaned back on hammock as it slowly rocked her and Hassan.

It was their second night on the island, and Promise had arranged for a private firework show to kick off the eight-day trip.

"Yeah." Hassan nodded slowly, sensing something was off with Promise but turned his attention back to the projector that played a movie neither of them were really paying attention to as he too waited for the fireworks.

"Mrs. Davis, the show will begin in two minutes," one of the few staff that worked their island announced.

"Thank you." Promise smiled before moving from her seat to Hassan's, resting her head on his chest as he pulled her close, placing his hand on her round ass.

Exactly two minutes from being told the show would

start, fireworks began to color the sky as a video of their pictures crossed the screen. Hassan smiled at the memories.

Promise sat with an unreadable look. Hassan saw pictures he never knew had been taken, but each picture made him smile widely. The fireworks subsided as an image of Promise appeared. It was a video.

"Baby, I love you more than you can imagine. You made me your wife, so baby, I am making you a father," Hassan heard loud and clear.

"Wh-What?" he stuttered, sitting up, causing Promise to do so too.

Hassan looked from the projector to Promise, back to the projector. When he did, the video flipped to a still picture of Promise holding an ultrasound picture. The words under the picture read, *Daddy, I can't wait to meet you. I will be making my grand entrance September 2013.*

"I'm pregnant," Promise nervously announced the obvious.

The pair were quiet as they stared at each other. The only noise were the fireworks that had started again once the video was over. Without a word, Hassan leaned in, touching the side of Promise's face, bringing her lips close to his before kissing her deeply.

"Are you mad?" she asked once the kiss broke, and he just stared in her eyes.

"Nah, baby. Not even a little bit." Hassan smiled, showcasing his perfect, white teeth.

"You're my wife, the love of my life, and now, you're pregnant with my baby." He kissed her again.

Promise didn't imagine being pregnant this early on in their marriage, but after he proposed, the use of condoms went out the window, so they weren't exactly preventing it either.

Hassan kissed Promise again. It all made sense—her getting sick, not wanting to drink, and the nervousness.

"I love you." His voice was low and raspy as he stared in her eyes.

"I love you more." That smile that Hassan always caused crept slowly on her face.

Chapter
Forty-Nine

September 5th, 2013

Promise slowly walked out of the room of one of her patients. She was two days past her due date and in serious pain. Hassan had been trying to get her to stop working, but because Promise wasn't one to sit still, she just couldn't, even being nine months pregnant.

Before leaving the house today, Hassan begged her not to go in, but because her doctor told her she probably wouldn't go into labor for at least two more days, she went in anyway. Promise slowed her motion even more when she felt a sharp pain in the pit of her stomach. The Braxton Hicks were getting worse.

"Everything okay, Nurse Montgomery?" Dr. Whipple asked just as he was about to walk past Promise but saw the look of pain on her face.

"Yeah. Yeah, everything is fine." She lied.

Dr. Whipple was just about to say okay and keep it moving when he noticed an off look in her eyes.

"Hey, why don't you go ahead home for the day. It's slow in here anyway," he suggested.

"One of the other nurses can take over for you," he added.

Normally, Promise would have declined, but from the pain she was feeling all throughout her stomach, she knew needed to be home with her feet propped up as Hassan massaged them and she rested.

"Okay." She exhaled deeply as she felt another Braxton Hicks contraction. This one causing her to double over.

"Did yo—" He started, looking down.

"Water just break?" Promise finished as she looked down too and saw her gray scrub bottoms soaked as she stood in a puddle of water.

"Ummm, can you call Hassan?" Promise was calm, calmer than she thought she would be.

"Right away," Dr. Whipple said, hurrying away.

"I guess today is baby day," Promise whispered to herself.

"PUSH, BABY." Hassan encouraged as he held one of Promise's legs while a nurse held the other.

He looked down, watching and waiting for his first child to enter the world. It had only been forty-five minutes since Promise's water broke, and had it not been for Hassan being close to the hospital, he may have missed the birth.

For a first-time mom, Promise had progressed in no time.

"Come on, sweetheart. I can see hair." Marilyn gushed with tears as she stood near Promise's feet.

Promise exhaled deeply but jumped right back into pushing once she caught her breath. The pain was real, the contractions felt like a ton of bricks were crushing her body, and her vagina burned from feeling like it was being split a mile long, but Promise handled every pain like a champ.

"Keep going, baby. Keep going." Hassan's voice was filled with joy as it also cracked at the sight of his baby's head between Promise's thighs.

Giving it one last push, Promise pushed their baby. The doctor sat the crying baby on Promise's chest as she cried, looking down at the beautiful baby she and Hassan created.

"It's a girl, baby." Promise smiled with tears rolling as she looked up Hassan, who was crying himself.

Before this moment, neither one of them knew the sex of the baby. But hearing it was a girl made the moment so much more special for them.

"Dad, would you like to cut the cord?" the doctor asked, handing him the scissors without waiting for answer from him.

One of the nurses took their baby girl from them to clean him up, and Hassan leaned down to kiss Promise.

"I love you." He stroked the top of her head.

"I love you more." Her voice came off as a whisper as she reached up, gently wiping his tears as he always did her.

Hassan was her protector and provider, and she knew he would be the same for their daughter. Just like he protected her, she knew her king needed protecting too. She gently wiped his tears again. She would forever protect her king.

Life was perfect for Promise. She couldn't ask for anything better. She was the true definition of not letting your past define who you are.

ABOUT THE AUTHOR

Author Cherish Amore was born and raised in Williamsburg, Virginia. Ever since an early age, she used words to express her inner emotions as she explored freestyle poetry. It was during that phase of her life that she learned the importance of words, the weight and true power that feelings on paper could portray. What started off as therapeutic and an outlet for her, turned into a passion for the craft of creative writing. Hearing feedback and observing how her words moved people was fuel for her to pursue her passion. Her style of writing is very personal, and she wants the reader to relate to her stories and feel as if she took the words right out of their heart.

At 27, she felt that she had experienced a lot in her life and finally decided that it was time to, yet again, put her emotions on paper. She dug deep into her inner history, her most dark secrets, and bright smiles as she penned her first novel. She states that she hopes her story can help someone who may be going down the same road or merely pondering at the fork. She hopes that her story moves readers in the right direction and maybe inspires someone to pen out their own experiences in life.

To date she has penned, *A Perfect Harmonie 1 & 2, Not My Mother's Footsteps, When He's Too Good to Be True, An Imperfect Love Ruined Perfectly, Loving an Undercover,* and *Different Walks of Life Joined as One,* and she also co-wrote *Fighting for Love* and *Sleeping with My Daughter's Man.*

When Cherish Amore isn't writing, she enjoys singing,

reading, shopping, couponing, and spending time with her son, daughter, and husband, making memories.

If you have any questions, Cherish Amore can be reached at:

Email: CherishAmore@hotmail.com

ALSO BY CHERISH AMORE

Leap of Love

Behind These Eyes

Learning to Love